MEN'S BREAKFAST CLUB:
Blood, Faith and Fire

Abu Bakr Shareef

Men's Breakfast Club: Blood, Faith and Fire
Copyright © 2025 by Abu Bakr Shareef

Dedication

For the ones who stayed,

even when it got quiet, complicated, or cold.

For the ones who kept building

when the blueprints burned.

For the sisters who led without permission,

and the brothers who followed with humility.

And for every child who's still watching—

we didn't forget you.

This is for all of us.

Acknowledgments

To Allah—who gave me the breath to write, the wisdom to pause, and the strength to begin again. All praise is due to You.

To my family—thank you for your patience, your love, and your belief in the version of me that still needed time to arrive.

To the brothers who inspired these pages—you know who you are. Your stories, your scars, your silence, and your laughter shaped every chapter. I'm just the scribe.

To the sisters—who have always been the backbone of our communities, even when history tried to write you out. This book carries your fingerprints.

To the readers—thank you for walking with me. Through the fire, through the doubt, through the faith that refused to go out.

And to everyone still trying to heal while holding others—

You are the revolution.

Preface

Blood, Faith & Fire uses the spark of the first book to dive deeper into the hearts and habits of the men who make up the Breakfast Club. This time around, the cost of leadership, brotherhood, and faith is steeper. Decisions carry more weight. Consequences linger. And love—whether romantic, paternal, or spiritual—demands more than just good intentions.

Writing this sequel was not about tying up loose ends. It was about pulling the thread further—letting it unravel so the real conversations could begin. We're talking about revolution that turns on itself. About marriages that bend and break under pressure. About fatherhood with no manual and movements that ask too much.

This book is for anyone who's ever tried to do the right thing while standing in the middle of the fire. It's for the quiet leaders, the burdened husbands, the unsure revolutionaries, and the hopeful skeptics. It's for those who know that every man walks with contradictions and that growth often comes wrapped in pain.

Welcome to the next chapter. Step into the heat.

Abu Bakr Shareef

Table of Contents

Chapter One

Return of the Routine

I don't know what it is about quiet mornings that make you feel like things are finally falling into place—but I knew better than to trust the silence. Silence, for men like me, was never a sign of peace. It was a warning shot. A calm before the breaking. Life has a way of letting you get a few peaceful days in before chaos taps you on the shoulder like, "Hey big head."

Still, I tried to enjoy it. Tried to lean into the slow hum of sunrise prayers and the soft rustle of my kids breathing in the next room. I'd taken to making chai just before Fajr, a small ritual that gave me something to hold onto—literally and spiritually. The steam rising from the cup felt like proof that I was still standing, even if everything else around me was shifting.

After the whirlwind of betrayal, bullets, and birthing twins, you'd think things would slow down. They didn't. Not really. But I did. At least, I tried to. The mall incident was still fresh in my mind—flashes of broken glass, screaming, the smell of blood and fear. Sometimes, in the middle of the night, I'd wake up gasping, my heart racing like I'd just sprinted through the scene again.

Bronx was finally back on his feet. Somewhat. The man had always carried pain like it was an accessory, something he wore but never spoke about. Even now, after everything, he walked like he was still dodging invisible bullets. I watched him closely. His laugh would start strong, then stutter halfway through, like a record skipping. His eyes drifted off mid-conversation, zoning out into spaces I couldn't follow.

But he was trying. That was more than I could say for some.

He'd started shadowing gym classes at a local charter school—something that gave him structure, a little purpose. I saw glimpses of the old Bronx in the way he held the clipboard, how he corrected a kid's squat form like it was life or death. His body was strong again. His shoulders filled out his hoodie, and he moved with that athletic grace that used to turn heads. But his mind? Still navigating a battlefield I couldn't see.

He showed up to my house every so often, mostly unannounced, usually around dinnertime. He never said it outright, but I think he just wanted to see life happening. Kids laughing. A wife humming in the kitchen. A baby spitting up on your shirt while you're trying to make wudu. All the things that made life messy and loud and real.

Sara had developed a system with the boys that made our house feel like a well-oiled daycare center. Every diaper change was a scheduled mission. Naps? Coordinated like a NASA launch. Feedings? Strategic. And Imani—bless her little heart—was in full big-sister mode, offering pacifiers like bribes and declaring herself "Team No Boys" anytime one of the twins cried too loud.

I stayed out of the way. I'd learned the hard way that Sara's zone was sacred. She ran the house like a military compound with the tenderness of a lioness guarding her cubs. My role? Official errand man, prayer rug cleaner, and late-night snack fetcher. It wasn't a glamorous life, but I loved it. Even if my back hurt and I hadn't heard complete silence in three months.

I think that's what saved me. The routine. The boring, blessed normalcy. That, and the chai.

It was a Thursday morning when I sat staring at the group chat thread, thumb hovering over the screen like the text I was about to send could shift the Earth. The group had been quiet. Too quiet. Sure, a few memes and voice notes trickled in now and then—usually Ameer going off about gas prices or Kareem sending clips from old Malcolm speeches—but there was no spark. No center.

The last time we were all in one place, the room had too much tension. I could still hear the echo of that final argument. Too many visions. Too many egos. Too many scars that never got treated.

I sighed, then typed the message.

Sunday. 9:30 a.m. Brunch spot on Heights. No speeches. Just brothers and food.

I didn't expect much. Maybe Bronx. Maybe Ameer. But one by one, replies started lighting up the screen like little neon signs of hope.

Ameer: "If there's chicken and waffles, count me in."

Kareem: "Y'all know I don't wake up early… but for this, I'll set the alarm."

Bronx: "I'll be there. I got thoughts."

Even Abdul, the ghost of our crew, texted: "Say less."

By Saturday night, I was ironing a button-down shirt. That's how I knew I was serious. Not for fashion, but for honor. These men had seen me cry, fight, fall. They'd seen me break. But they were still my brothers.

Sunday morning came like a soft drumbeat in the chest. I left the house early. Told Sara I just needed some air before the brunch. She gave me that nod—the one that says "I see you" without making a speech. Her support came quiet and consistent, the way rivers cut stone.

I parked a block away from the Heights Café. Didn't want to pull up too fast. Wanted to take it in—feel what the morning felt like when something sacred was about to start again. I sipped my chai in the car for a few minutes before stepping out. The air was crisp, but not cold. The kind of breeze that made your lungs feel new.

One by one, the brothers pulled up. Ameer was first, wearing a mustard yellow hoodie and sandals like he'd just come from a TED Talk on soul food. Kareem arrived with his kufi tilted sideways, always halfway between cool and conscious. Bronx came quiet, eyes scanning everything like he couldn't turn off the part of him that stayed ready. Then Abdul, Bluetooth in ear, looking like he just closed a multi-million-dollar contract from his Honda Accord.

"Y'all missed me, huh?" he grinned, dapping up the whole table like we were a rap group reuniting for a world tour. "I came to see if y'all still got vision… or if y'all just washed."

We all laughed. Real laughter. The kind that made your shoulders drop and your spirit lift.

We ordered heavy. French toast, jerk salmon, halal chicken and waffles, the whole brunchy spread. As the food came out, so did the stories. We talked about jobs. Parenting. Marriage. Politics. Faith. That weird tension of being Black and Muslim in a world that still doesn't quite know what to do with either.

I mostly listened at first. Just let the voices roll over me. Bronx talked about shadowing at the school, how one of the kids reminded him of his younger self—full of rage but hungry for a reason to believe in something. Ameer confessed he'd been in therapy for the last three months and that he'd started journaling again. Kareem shared that he was working with a small group on prison re-entry programs for Muslim brothers who got locked up young and thrown away early.

Even Abdul, behind all his slick jokes and brand-name drops, admitted his marriage was hanging by a thread. Said he'd been so busy "building the empire" that he didn't realize his queen had emotionally moved out six months ago.

That one sat heavy.

I pushed my plate away. "Maybe we were moving too fast before," I said quietly. "All this talk about movements and building and revolutions—we skipped over checking our own foundations."

The table got still. Ameer nodded. Bronx looked down. Kareem leaned back. Nobody interrupted.

"I still believe in what we were doing," Bronx said. "But maybe we forgot to build the brotherhood before we built the brand."

"Exactly," I replied. "We went corporate before we went communal. I don't want another movement. I want a mission. A core. Something small and real. Something we can explain in one sentence. Something we can live, not just fundraise for."

Abdul cocked his head. "What's the sentence then?"

I didn't answer right away. I just let the silence speak for me. Then I said it.

"We serve our people with our faith as the blueprint."

No one clapped. No one hit me with a "BarakAllahu feek." Just slow nods. Sips of tea. That was enough.

We stayed another hour, but there were no photos. No speeches. Just hugs at the end and quiet promises to meet again in two weeks.

At home, Sara was wiping down the kitchen counters. The twins were asleep. Imani was coloring a picture of a unicorn with a hijab. I slid off my shoes and walked into that chaos-turned-peace.

"How'd it go?" Sara asked without looking up.

"Simple," I said. "No drama. No agenda. Just brothers breaking bread."

She nodded and smiled faintly, her hand never stopping. "Sounds like the beginning of something solid."

I didn't respond. Just exhaled and leaned against the doorway, watching her work. Watching this life we'd built out of broken bricks and borrowed breath. Maybe it was the return of the routine. Or maybe, just maybe, it was something better.

A foundation built to last.

There were moments in the middle of the night when I'd lie awake, staring at the ceiling, wondering what parts of myself I'd left behind in the chaos of the past year. Sometimes I'd hear one of the twins crying through the monitor, and I'd get up to check, but it wasn't really the crying that woke me. It was the weight. The kind you don't talk about in the group chat. The kind that lives in your chest like a roommate who never pays rent.

I'd tiptoe past Sara's side of the bed, careful not to wake her. She had her own weight to carry, and she did it with more grace than I ever could. I'd look down at the boys in their crib, wrapped like little burritos, chests rising and falling in perfect rhythm. It always hit me hard then—how much I didn't know. How much I feared messing them up. How little I felt equipped to raise Black Muslim sons in a world that barely made space for either identity.

Sometimes, after checking on the boys, I'd just sit in the hallway and stare at the door. Imani had decorated it with drawings and stickers—little hearts, sparkly butterflies, a crookedly drawn "Welcome to Big Sister Club" sign. That door reminded me of how quickly life could stretch you. One day you're trying to figure out who you are, and the next you're responsible for tiny lives and a household full of expectations.

Bronx had a similar look in his eyes at brunch that Sunday. The kind of look you only get when you've been to war and returned with invisible shrapnel. He didn't speak much at first, just watched. His shoulders were tense, but his hands trembled slightly when he lifted his glass. I noticed it, even if no one else did.

During a lull in conversation, I leaned toward him and asked, "You been sleeping better?"

He gave a half shrug, then stared at his plate. "Not really. Dreams come in loud. Like sirens. Ain't even dreams half the time. Just reruns of that night."

We both knew what he meant.

"I feel that," I said. "My peace still got a limp."

That made him chuckle, just a little. "You ever think we're not supposed to have peace? Like… maybe this world don't want men like us healed?"

I sipped my tea slowly. "Maybe. Or maybe peace ain't a destination. Maybe it's a practice. Like salat. You don't do it once and say, 'I'm good forever.' You gotta return to it. Daily. Even when it feels pointless."

"Especially when it feels pointless," he said, nodding.

The others had drifted into a side conversation about the mayoral elections and some drama in the local masjid board, but Bronx and I sat in that quieter lane. That back row of brotherhood where the real stuff gets whispered.

"Ever think about quitting?" he asked suddenly.

"Quitting what?"

"All of it. The group. The community. This… leadership life. Just being a regular brother with no inbox full of people needing something."

"Every week," I said without missing a beat.

He smiled again. "But you stay."

"So do you."

That was the thing. We could complain, threaten to walk away, even ghost each other for weeks—but somehow, we always came back. That's what the world didn't understand. Brotherhood wasn't about perfection. It was about return.

Kareem leaned over from his end of the table. "I know we said no speeches, but real talk—this brunch is healing. I didn't realize how bad I needed to be around y'all."

Ameer nodded. "Same. I been around people, but not my people. Not in this way."

Abdul, who had been uncharacteristically quiet, set down his fork and looked up. "Y'all ever feel like… we were trying to build a table for our people, but we never built chairs for ourselves?"

That landed heavy.

"I been sitting on the floor spiritually," he continued. "Making room for everybody else while my own soul got callouses."

We didn't respond right away. Sometimes silence is the most honest reply.

"I'm tired of performing," Kareem said. "Tired of pretending to have all the answers just because I memorize a few ayat. I need space to be unsure. Space to wrestle."

Bronx grunted. "Ain't that the truth. This deen got beauty, but some days, all I got is bruises."

I could feel the layers of performance peeling off around the table. The armor, the pride, the curated images—all loosening like the top button after a heavy meal. We were getting to the truth. And it wasn't always pretty.

"I think," I said, voice steady but soft, "that we've been acting like we need to lead something big to feel like men. But maybe we just need to lead something true. Even if it's small."

Ameer looked at me, eyes shining. "You saying I can be a revolutionary and still rock baby spit-up on my hoodie?"

I smirked. "Only if the hoodie's ethically sourced."

That got a round of laughs, the kind that cracked open the shell of tension we'd all been wearing. In that moment, it felt like we weren't just reconnecting—we were being rebuilt. By truth. By tea. By testimony.

As we wrapped up, we split the bill evenly, no arguments. That was a miracle in itself. Abdul stood and adjusted his watch. "Alright y'all. Two weeks?"

"Two weeks," I confirmed.

"Same place?"

"Maybe somewhere new," I said. "New place. Same purpose."

We hugged each other like it was Eid. Not the rushed, surface-level dap hugs, but the full embrace—the kind that says, "I see you. I need you. I got you."

Back home, after Sara asked how it went and I gave her the usual "simple" reply, I wandered into the living room. Imani had fallen asleep on the couch, arms wrapped around a plush unicorn. The TV was still playing soft Quran recitation in the background.

I sat for a long time.

Staring. Praying. Processing.

That brunch wasn't just a catch-up. It was a reset. A reminder. That even when the world feels broken and your faith feels thin and your purpose gets blurry, you still have brothers. You still have roots. You still have a God who welcomes you back without shame.

Maybe the routine wasn't just returning.

Maybe I was.

Chapter Two

Shadows in the Sunlight

Something was off with Sakeena.

You don't always need words. Sometimes you just know. The same way you sense a storm before it hits. A certain stillness in the air. A feeling in your gut that won't let you sit still. My daughter wasn't just going through something. She was disappearing behind a curtain I couldn't pull back.

Her texts had gotten shorter. Dryer. The emojis disappeared, and the time between replies grew longer. When we video called, she would angle the camera like she was hiding something—like her background held secrets, or maybe she did. Her voice was light but rushed. Her face smiled, but her eyes didn't. And I'd seen that look before. I'd seen it on men preparing to lie. On women enduring one more day. It was that subtle kind of exhaustion that crawls behind the skin and waits for someone to notice.

She had told us she was "taking time for herself," trying to heal from the divorce. I wanted to honor that. Healing isn't linear. But silence? Silence speaks.

Sakeena had always been expressive, layered, complicated in the most beautiful way—but never evasive. Even when she was a teenager, she'd come to me crying after breakups or bad grades or friend drama. She never held in too much. Now, though? It felt like she was underwater—still visible, still waving, but unreachable.

Rasheeda noticed it too. She didn't say anything dramatic at first. Just light remarks, side comments meant to sound casual.

"Did she sound tired to you?"

"Was that an echo on the call or did it sound like she was somewhere else?"

"Her background was different, right? That didn't look like an apartment."

I waved her off at first. Told myself it was just stress. That we were all still healing. That maybe she just needed a break from us, from everything. But the doubts didn't leave. They stayed quiet, sitting beside me in the car, climbing into bed with me at night, whispering through every unanswered message.

I think I was hoping to be wrong. Hoping that time would reveal something simple—a new job, a temporary stay with a friend, maybe even a silent retreat in the woods. But this didn't feel like a sabbatical.

It felt like avoidance.

It felt like shame.

The garage had become our makeshift therapy center. Bronx and I didn't need couches or clipboards. We needed punching bags and sweat, the kind of release that turned buried emotion into something physical. That day, the air was heavy with summer humidity, but we boxed anyway—gloves on, mouthguards in, the sound of fists echoing off the concrete walls.

I let him jab first. Bronx always led with aggression, even when he wasn't angry. He had this way of throwing a punch like he was throwing his past away—one trauma at a time.

We danced around the bag for a while before I finally spoke.

"You hear from her lately?"

He slowed. "Sakeena?"

I nodded, wiping my forehead with my wrist.

"Not directly," he grunted, ducking a jab. "She sends the occasional 'hope you're well' text, but nothing deep."

"You ever feel like…" I hesitated, not because I didn't know the words, but because I didn't want to hear them out loud. "Like something else is going on?"

He stopped moving, let the gloves drop to his sides. The pause was long enough to feel like a confession.

"I did at first," he admitted. "But I figured she was just working through it. We've all been through something heavy. She deserves space."

"She deserves safety too," I muttered, voice low.

Bronx leaned against the garage wall, breathing heavy. "You think she's in danger?"

"I don't know," I said. "But I know when someone's lying to themselves. And she's not just pulling away from us—she's disappearing."

He didn't respond right away. He just nodded slowly, like someone who'd seen too many people fade before they fell.

"You want me to check in on her?"

I shook my head. "Nah. If it's time for someone to go, it should be me."

I didn't tell Sara everything.

That night, I kissed the twins on the forehead and told her I had business in Dallas. It wasn't a lie—there were some nonprofit contacts I needed to reconnect with—but that wasn't the real reason. I didn't lie to her. I just didn't unfold the full truth. Some truths are too raw to say out loud until you've survived them.

She didn't press. She just placed a small travel prayer mat in my bag, kissed my cheek, and whispered, "Come back with peace."

I left early the next morning, driving through open stretches of road with nothing but old school Nas playing low through the speakers. It gave me space to think. To plan. To brace myself.

By the time I got to the address Sakeena had given us two months ago, the sun was setting behind scattered clouds, casting long shadows across the street. I parked outside the complex and walked to the leasing office, unsure of what I even planned to say.

The woman behind the desk smiled politely until I mentioned the name.

"Oh, Sakeena," she said, typing into her system. "She moved out… let me see… a little over five weeks ago."

I kept my expression still, nodded once. "Did she leave a forwarding address?"

She shook her head. "Afraid not."

I thanked her and walked back to the car, each step heavier than the last. I sat there with the engine off, hands on the steering wheel, chest tight.

I didn't call Sakeena. I didn't even text. I just sat in the silence and let the possibilities churn in my mind like a storm. I knew she wasn't in danger—not the physical kind. But something was being hidden, and that was worse. Because when people hide, it's usually from the ones they love most.

The phone rang before I could even start the ignition.

Rasheeda.

"She's not where she said she was," I said as soon as I answered.

A beat of silence.

"Then where is she?" her voice trembled.

"I don't know," I admitted. "But I'm going to find out."

It didn't take long to track her down.

I still had a few contacts in the Dallas area—old friends, school connections, one or two masjid board members who owed me a favor. I made a few discreet calls. Mentioned her name carefully. No pressure. Just checking in. Concerned parent stuff.

Most people said the same thing: "Haven't seen her lately," or "She posted something a while ago, but nothing recent."

But one call slipped.

A brother who ran a weekend youth halaqah let it slip that someone had seen her in a different part of the city. A wealthier area. The kind of neighborhood where the homes looked like magazine covers and every driveway had a car that cost more than my annual salary. It was the sort of place you don't end up in unless you're very intentional—or being kept.

I drove there without a plan.

I just needed to see her.

I told myself I wasn't there to spy or confront or accuse. But a father knows better than to believe his own lies.

I spotted her before I even pulled onto the block.

She was standing outside a large, modern home—gated, manicured, pristine. The house looked like it belonged in a tech entrepreneur's dream journal. And there she was, in jeans and a long sweater, her hijab wrapped in that soft turban style she favored when she was trying not to be noticed.

She was laughing.

Not loudly. But enough to make my chest tighten. She was talking to a man I didn't recognize. He looked older. Late thirties, maybe early forties. Tall. Stylish. Confident. His posture was relaxed, the kind of calm that came from wealth or power—or both. He handed her a tote bag and touched her elbow lightly. It wasn't flirtatious. But it was familiar.

The kind of touch that says, We've done this before.

I didn't get out of the car.

Didn't roll down the window.

I just watched.

She looked… happy.

But not the kind of happy that made you feel warm. It was curated. Performative. Her smile was wide, but her shoulders were too straight. Too stiff. Like someone playing a part for a role she hadn't rehearsed enough to own.

She didn't see me.

And I didn't make myself known.

I just sat there until they disappeared into the house, the gate closing quietly behind them like the scene had never happened.

I didn't go home.

I drove to the nearest masjid. It was almost Maghrib. The building was modest—faded carpet, dim lights, a leaky faucet in the wudu area—but it felt like shelter. I washed up slowly, letting the cold water rinse the anger from my hands. I prayed. Not out of clarity or strength. But out of desperation.

I begged Allah for guidance. For patience. For the words I didn't know how to say.

After the prayer, I sat in the back row alone.

I stared at the prayer rug for a long time.

Then I cried.

I didn't sob. I didn't make noise. Just slow, quiet tears—the kind that sneak out when your soul has finally lost the war it's been pretending it wasn't fighting.

Later that night, I called her.

"Just checking in," I said, voice low.

"Everything's fine, Baba," she replied too quickly. Too cleanly. "I've just been busy. Work and life, you know?"

"Where are you staying these days?"

"Still in the city," she said. "I moved into a new apartment. I'll send the address."

She didn't.

And I didn't push.

But I took note.

There's a certain point in parenthood when you stop trying to steer and start trying to trust. But trust has to be earned. And when someone lies to you with a smile, it leaves a wound you can't explain to anyone but God.

I got back home just before midnight.

The house was quiet. Dark except for the hallway nightlight and the soft hum of the baby monitor. Sara was asleep on the couch, wrapped in one of my old hoodies, a burp cloth on her shoulder like a badge of survival. The twins had worn her out again.

I watched her breathe for a moment.

There's something sacred about seeing the person you love at rest. It reminds you that even in the middle of chaos, some things are still whole. Still untouched. Still yours.

I took a shower, prayed 'Isha, then sat on the edge of the bed, too wired to sleep. My bag was still at the door, unopened. My phone was dark. My mind, though—it was running.

Sakeena's face kept flashing in my mind. The way she'd smiled. The way that man had touched her arm like it was normal. Like he had access.

Who was he?

What did he mean to her?

Why the lie?

The questions came in waves, crashing into my chest without warning. I didn't want to jump to conclusions, but I also couldn't shake the image. A gated house. A strange man. A forced smile.

And then—her voice. Soft. Distant. Careful.

"Everything's fine, Baba."

Everything wasn't fine. I knew it. And she knew I knew.

The next morning, life moved on like it always does.

Diapers. Bottles. Breakfast. Imani refusing to wear matching socks. Bronx came by later that afternoon to review the final steps in his certification process. We sat at the kitchen table with paperwork spread out between us and a pot of chai slowly cooling as the sun passed overhead.

"You alright?" he asked, halfway through signing a form.

"Yeah," I said.

He looked up. "You sure?"

I paused. Then nodded. "Not really."

Bronx didn't push. He never did. He just slid one of the forms closer and said, "Let's finish this. Then we talk."

So we did. One form at a time. A checklist that moved him closer to stability. To something like purpose.

Afterward, we sat in the backyard, watching Imani draw hopscotch squares on the concrete with chalk.

"You see her?" he asked finally.

"Yeah."

"She okay?"

I sighed. "She looks okay."

"But?"

"But it's an act. A pretty good one, but I know my daughter. Something's not right."

"You think she's in trouble?"

"Not yet," I said. "But I think she's in deeper than she can admit."

We didn't say much after that. Just watched the sky change color. Watched my daughter chase my granddaughter across the yard. Watched the world try to feel normal again.

In the days that followed, I tried to immerse myself in the movement again. We hosted another brunch with the brothers—this one smaller, quieter. We talked about re-entry programs, mentorship pipelines, even kicked around the idea of starting a monthly halaqah for young Black Muslim professionals who felt alienated in the masjid.

There were moments when I felt reconnected. Present. Needed.

But then, in the quiet moments, Sakeena's face would return. Her voice would echo. Her lie would replay.

At night, I'd wake up and check my phone for the address she never sent. And every time, it wasn't there.

Sara noticed my distraction. She didn't ask directly, but she held me longer during hugs. Made my tea stronger in the morning. Started sending me small hadith quotes through text like spiritual lifelines.

One of them hit hard.

"Whoever is not merciful to his child, Allah will not be merciful to him."

—[Sahih Bukhari]

I stared at that text for a long time.

Was I being harsh?

Or was I just scared?

The thing about fatherhood is… you never really stop parenting. You just move from controlling to guiding to praying. And sometimes, when your child lies to you with a smile, you realize the next phase has begun.

The phase where all you can do… is wait.

Sakeena wasn't lost.

But she was wandering.

And I knew, deep in my bones, that we hadn't seen the last of what this shadow would reveal.

Chapter Three

All Power, No Peace

Bilal was tired.

Not the kind of tired that a nap could cure—but the kind that seeped into the marrow of your soul. The kind of tired that made your shadow slouch. The kind of tired that made every breath feel like negotiation.

He looked smaller than I remembered. Not physically, but spiritually. As if the weight of too many battles had worn down his spine just enough to tilt him toward despair.

His thobe hung off him like it belonged to someone else. His beard had grown patchy and uneven, the edges fraying in quiet rebellion. His shoulders, usually squared like a soldier's, were now slightly hunched. There was no mistaking it—he was unraveling.

I hadn't seen him in nearly a month. We'd both been caught up in our own trenches—him launching the civil rights branch of Black Up, and me juggling fatherhood, local school board advocacy, Bronx's reintegration, and this slow-burning fear about Sakeena I hadn't yet named out loud.

When I finally made time to visit him, I found him in a storefront that looked more like a forgotten campaign office than a legal center. Tucked between a halal meat market and an abandoned barbershop, the windows were dusty and the blinds half-bent. But this was the new base of operations—the heartbeat of Bilal's revolution.

I stepped inside and was greeted not by a receptionist or a welcoming smile, but by silence and the scent of printer toner.

"Peace, brother," I said.

He didn't look up.

"Wa 'alaykum salaam," he murmured, fingers flying across his laptop keyboard.

The room was cluttered. Folders everywhere. A map of Texas pinned to the wall, with red markers stabbed into cities like wounds. The bookshelf held only Qur'ans, tax codes, and a single framed photo of Malcolm X. There was a fold-out table in the corner with two lukewarm water bottles and a half-eaten granola bar.

"Place looks lived in," I said, trying to inject a little lightness.

He smirked, still typing. "No receptionist. Can't afford one. Besides, folks don't show up unless they're mad. Then they find a way in."

I sat down across from him. "So. What's the update?"

That's when he stopped.

He leaned back in the chair and just… exhaled. That kind of long, slow breath that people take when they're fighting not to break.

"We're in over our heads. That's the update."

He wasn't exaggerating.

The civil rights initiative had started as a grassroots project—a legal support wing that could offer emergency help to families brutalized by police or wronged by racist systems. But word spread fast. Too fast.

Now it wasn't just Houston and Austin calling. There were messages from Chicago, Memphis, Atlanta, even Oakland. The inbox was flooded with voice notes from crying mothers and desperate fathers. People pleading for someone—anyone—to care.

Bilal grabbed a stack of manila folders and dropped them between us on the table with a thud.

"These people aren't clients," he said quietly. "They're casualties."

He opened the first folder—an eleven-year-old boy handcuffed by a school resource officer after he asked to use the bathroom twice in one class.

"They said he was being disruptive."

He flipped to the next—a woman whose wrists were broken by an overzealous TSA agent after she questioned why her scarf had to be removed.

"They said she was uncooperative."

Another folder—this one thin, but heavier than the rest. Inside: a single photo. A young man, no older than twenty-two, facedown in a hospital bed with a breathing tube and two shattered legs. His mother's hand rested on his back in the picture.

"Accused of resisting. No weapon. No record. Just ran from the wrong traffic stop."

Bilal looked up. His eyes were bloodshot. His voice had a tremble he tried to hide.

"I thought I had the muscle for this," he said. "Thought I could handle the strategy, the planning, the advocacy. But every day, it's like I'm dragging this whole thing through mud while someone's stepping on my neck."

"You're not dragging it," I said. "You're pulling people out of fires."

He shook his head. "I thought this would make me feel powerful. That's what they don't tell you—activism isn't power. It's paperwork. It's funerals. It's fundraising with a smile while your heart bleeds. I walk into courtrooms praying I don't get disrespected before I even open my mouth."

I could feel his exhaustion. I'd felt it myself in different forms. Community work always sounds noble until you're in it—until you're sacrificing your marriage, your health, your sleep, and your silence just to be heard by systems that never intended to listen.

He leaned over and pulled out a folded letter from under his laptop. His fingers shook slightly.

"Remember that Dallas case? The little boy who was slammed against the lockers?"

I nodded, jaw tight.

"They closed the investigation. Said the officer's use of force was 'within policy.' The internal memo said it was 'regrettable but justified.'"

"Qualified immunity?" I asked, already knowing the answer.

"Always."

"And the family?"

"Devastated. The father wants to burn the precinct down. Literally. He told me if he can't get justice through us, he'll get it with gasoline."

We sat in silence for a long time.

Just breathing.

The sound of a passing bus outside broke the stillness. Somewhere down the block, a car horn blared. Life moved on, but we stayed suspended— two men staring into a pile of pain, wondering if anything we built could outlast the grief.

"What do you want to do?" I asked finally.

Bilal leaned back in his chair, rubbed his temples with both hands, and stared at the ceiling like it owed him answers.

"Part of me wants to walk away," he said. "Pack it all up. Disappear. Let the whole movement fall if it means I get to sleep again."

"And the other part?" I asked.

He paused. His voice dropped to a whisper.

"The other part wants to burn everything down. Shut down courtrooms, chain myself to police stations, flip every table in every city until they take us seriously."

There it was—the rage. The holy fire that fuels so many movements but destroys so many men.

I leaned forward, elbows on my knees. "You want a revolution. I get that. But revolutions without roots? They collapse. Loud doesn't always mean listened to. You don't want to torch the village and realize you were living in it too."

He nodded slowly, breathing through his nose.

"So what's the play then?"

"We pick one case," I said. "Just one. One we can win. We document it. Build momentum. Use it to fundraise. Build a platform off truth, not trauma."

"Which case?" he asked.

"The boy from Dallas. He's still alive. Still able to speak. That's a witness and a face. Start there."

Bilal stared at me. The spark returned behind his eyes—dim but present.

"You sound like the professor," he muttered.

I smiled. "Well, he did try to get us to plan before preaching."

He smirked, then stood. "Thank you. For showing up."

I gripped his shoulder. "Always. Just don't forget—nobody builds a movement alone."

He looked like he wanted to say more, maybe even cry, but then—my phone buzzed.

Rasheeda.

A text lit the screen:

"Call me ASAP. It's about Sakeena."

My heart dropped into my stomach.

Bilal saw my face change and didn't ask. He just stepped aside.

I left the office fast, the folders and cases still open behind me like unfinished prayers.

The sun had dipped low, and the city was starting to hum with that late-afternoon restlessness. People leaving work. Headlights flickering on. Horns and sirens in the distance like a song you couldn't dance to.

I sat in the car, staring at the phone before I called.

What now? What else?

I pressed her name.

She answered on the first ring.

"Please tell me you're sitting down," Rasheeda said, voice shaking.

"I'm listening."

"It's about Sakeena. Someone just called me. Someone I didn't expect. And what they told me—"

She stopped.

"What is it, Rasheeda?"

"I think… I think she's involved with someone. And it's not good. And it's not new."

My mouth went dry.

"I need details," I said, starting the car.

"I'll tell you everything. But… this might not be a conversation for the phone."

I pulled out of the parking lot and into the street, the weight of two worlds crashing into each other—my role as a leader trying to help save a people, and my role as a father trying not to lose his daughter.

It was time to choose.

Bilal had always been the one with the fire.

Back when we first started Black Up, he was the one crashing city council meetings with printed stats, handing out flyers to strangers at gas stations, organizing 3 a.m. rides to courthouse vigils. His passion was magnetic. He made you feel like change wasn't just possible—it was mandatory.

I remembered one night, maybe five years ago, when we drove six hours to stand outside a jail in a town nobody had ever heard of, just because a Black Muslim teen had been arrested without bail after defending himself from a racial slur. We stood in the cold with six other protestors while Bilal led a dhikr circle and then gave a speech straight from the gut. He didn't even have a mic—just his voice, raw and cracking, echoing off the concrete.

He told us then: "We don't show up because it's convenient. We show up because it's sacred."

I held onto that line for years. Quoted it in lectures. Posted it on flyers. But sitting in that office now, watching the same man tremble over an inbox he could no longer manage, I wondered if sacredness was still enough.

"We were supposed to be bigger than this," he said. "We had a vision. A blueprint. Remember the summit we planned? The citywide mobilization strategy?"

"I remember," I said softly.

He stared out the window.

"Now I can't even keep my lights on unless I take speaking gigs I don't believe in. I smile on panels next to imams who won't even say Black Lives Matter in khutbahs."

"That's not on you."

He turned back. "But I let it happen. I let this thing get branded. Sanitized. Now they want a civil rights movement they can sponsor—one that won't get too loud or too Black."

"You didn't let anything happen," I said. "You kept it alive."

He laughed bitterly. "Barely."

I leaned forward. "Then let's start fresh. Quietly. Not a march. Not a press release. A case. A story. A win."

He was quiet for a long time. Then finally—he nodded.

And just as hope started to settle in my chest—Rasheeda's text shattered it.

Here is the final section of Chapter Three: All Power, No Peace, completing the expansion to hit the 4,000-word target. This section heightens the emotional cliffhanger involving Sakeena and deepens the narrator's internal conflict.

The line was quiet for a beat. Just Rasheeda's breath.

"Who called you?" I asked.

"You remember Sister Anisa from the Dallas Muslim health collective?" she said. "She and I were in a wellness circle last year. We haven't talked in months, but she called out of nowhere."

"And?"

"She said she saw Sakeena. At a private event. A dinner hosted at a donor's house for Muslim professionals."

That didn't sound so bad.

"Okay. That's not necessarily—"

"She was on his arm."

I stopped breathing for a second.

"Whose arm?"

Rasheeda hesitated. "A man. Older. Divorced. Wealthy. Known in the community but not known, if you get what I mean. He runs in political circles. Donates a lot to masjids but doesn't go to many. She said it looked… personal."

The image flashed in my mind—Sakeena at the gated house, the tote bag, the soft touch on the elbow. It all connected.

"Did Anisa speak to her?"

"She tried. But Sakeena just gave her this strange smile. Said she was doing 'private work' and had to leave early."

I leaned back against the seat, hand on my chest.

"I don't want to assume," I said. "But this… this isn't her. She's never been this secretive."

"Maybe it's trauma," Rasheeda offered. "After everything with the divorce…"

I nodded, even though she couldn't see it.

But I knew.

This wasn't trauma alone.

This was choice.

And that's what scared me.

That night, I didn't sleep.

Sara noticed. She didn't ask. She just held my hand in the dark and let the silence stretch between us. I appreciated that.

Sometimes the most faithful thing your partner can do is wait with you.

I lay there thinking about all the nights I carried Sakeena on my shoulders during family hikes, how she'd ask questions about the stars and the Prophets, how she once told her second-grade class she wanted to be a scholar and a scientist because "Allah made my brain big enough for both."

Where did that little girl go?

And how much of her did I lose by trying to raise a daughter who didn't disappoint her father, instead of raising a woman strong enough to define her own dignity?

The next morning, I called Kareem.

He was the only one in the circle who could track someone discreetly—legally and spiritually.

"I'm not asking you to spy," I told him. "Just… if you hear her name, let me know. I'm not trying to control her. I just need to make sure this isn't going somewhere dangerous."

Kareem was silent for a moment.

"You're scared," he said.

"I am."

"Then you're still her father. That counts for something."

Later that day, I sat with Bronx on the porch. The twins were napping. Imani was in the yard, blowing bubbles and pretending they were invisible force fields.

Bronx sipped his tea and studied my face.

"Your head's somewhere else," he said.

"Sakeena."

He nodded slowly. "You gonna talk to her?"

"I want to. But I want to go in with wisdom. Not fear."

"That's the thing about daughters," he said. "They want freedom. But they still need faith that their father will be there when they fall."

I exhaled hard. "I just don't want to find out too late."

"You won't," he said. "Because you're already looking."

Chapter Four

Shadows and Secrets

Sakeena was missing.

Not in the sirens-and-search-party kind of way, but in the quieter, more haunting way—the way someone slowly fades out of the frame until you realize they've been gone longer than you want to admit.

Three days. No calls. No texts. No social media activity. Her phone rang once, then straight to voicemail. By the time Rasheeda called me, her voice shook like she was holding back a scream.

"She's not at the apartment," she said from the front seat of her car. I could hear the wind rushing through a cracked window. "Sahara said they were supposed to meet for brunch. She never showed."

"She's not answering me either," I said, pacing the hallway. "I thought maybe she just needed space again. But something's off."

"Bronx doesn't know anything. I asked him too."

That got my attention.

I knew Bronx had always kept a quiet but protective eye on her, especially after the divorce. He never crossed boundaries, but he checked in—small things, like food drop-offs, random texts, invites to events she usually declined. If even he didn't know where she was, this wasn't just a mood swing.

This was deliberate.

"I'm scared, Jibril," Rasheeda whispered.

That made two of us.

I told her to stay put. I didn't want two people driving around emotional. I'd handle the first leg.

I grabbed my keys and jacket and headed for the place I swore I'd never show up to without an invitation—Sakeena's apartment. She had drawn a line around that space. Her sacred ground. Her retreat from all our well-meaning plans for her.

"This is my space to feel like me," she told me once, sitting across from me at brunch, eyes firm. "Not your daughter. Not Rasheeda's legacy. Just… me."

I respected that. I gave her the space.

But now? Space felt like a luxury I could no longer afford.

The complex looked tired. Wrought-iron gates that hadn't closed properly in years. A buzzer that rang like a mosquito with asthma. I parked near her car—a beat-up Toyota Camry with one hubcap missing and a cracked bumper sticker that read Dissent is Divine.

Her car was there.

That didn't make me feel better.

I knocked twice, waited, then tried the door.

It opened.

Unlocked.

And that's when my stomach turned.

The door creaked open like a warning.

Not dramatic.

Just enough to make me pause.

The hallway was still. The kind of still that makes you question your own breath. I stepped inside slowly, calling her name.

"Sakeena?"

No answer.

The apartment smelled faintly of oud and mint tea. Her scent. Her rhythm. That delicate balance between soft and strong. I moved through the living room carefully, as if walking through someone else's prayer.

The lights were off. Curtains drawn. No signs of struggle, but no signs of comfort either. Her favorite incense burner on the bookshelf had gone cold. The plants near the window were wilting from neglect.

I checked the bedroom.

Bed unmade. Qur'an open on the dresser, a soft purple tasbih resting between pages like a bookmark for her soul. A glass of water half-full on the nightstand. And on the desk, her journal—closed. Untouched.

But no daughter.

I sat down on the edge of her bed. That's when it hit me—this was the first time I had ever been inside this apartment. And it felt like a museum of someone who had disappeared on purpose.

How did we get here?

Had I really been so busy—organizing brothers, planning strategies, coordinating workshops—that I didn't notice my own child slipping away?

I looked at her books. Sociology, Islamic ethics, poetry collections with dog-eared corners. A photo of her with Imani on Eid day, both in matching lavender hijabs, grinning wide. My daughter. My firstborn. The one who used to fall asleep on my chest during late-night halaqahs when she was just five.

A memory pushed its way to the surface.

One night, years ago, we were driving home from a community fundraiser.

She was barely nine, sitting in the backseat, wide-eyed and quiet.

"Baba," she said suddenly. "If you help everybody else… who helps you?"

I didn't answer right away. I remember being surprised by the question. I told her something generic. Something about Allah helping those who help others.

But now, sitting here in her absence, I realized what she was really asking:

Will there still be enough of you left for me?

That night, I brushed it off.

Tonight, I wasn't so sure.

On her desk was a small envelope with my name on it. My full name, in her handwriting—"Baba – Jibril."

I opened it slowly.

Inside: a short note.

Baba, don't worry. I need time. I'll be okay, in sha Allah. Please don't come looking for me. Trust me. Love you.

No address. No phone number. No explanation.

I stared at the note for a long time before I remembered to breathe.

Then I took a photo and sent it to Rasheeda.

My phone buzzed immediately: "We need to find her."

I agreed. But first, I needed help.

Twenty minutes later, Bilal pulled into the lot in his dented Corolla, parked two spaces down from mine, and climbed out with a laptop under one arm, a flash drive in his pocket, and a bottle of zamzam water clutched tight like it was a weapon.

"I prayed istikhara on the way," he said before I even greeted him.

His eyes were sharper than usual. Focused. Wary. He looked at me the way soldiers look at each other before entering a house they might not come out of.

"You sure she left willingly?" he asked as we stepped inside.

"I think so," I said. "But that doesn't mean she's safe."

He nodded once and sat at her desk, booting up the laptop. "Let's see what we can find."

I paced while he worked, hands clenched behind my back, my heart thudding with every keystroke he made. He moved quickly—checking her email servers, encrypted backups, cloud logins. Most were empty or dormant.

"She scrubbed it," he said, not even looking up. "Cleared her search history, deleted all cookies, disabled location sharing."

"She covered her tracks?"

He leaned back. "She did better than that. She made it look like she was never here."

I sat down on the floor. Not the chair. The floor.

There's something about the moment you realize your child has learned to hide from you—and that you taught her how, by example. I'd spent my life moving in and out of activism like a ghost. I'd trained myself to disappear. Now my daughter had inherited the art of absence.

"You know…" Bilal started slowly, "there's one person who could find her. If we really wanted to."

I didn't even look up. I already knew where he was going.

"No."

"Just hear me out."

"No, Bilal."

"We don't bring snakes back into the garden."

He stared at me. "He's not a snake. He's a python. And sometimes, if you want to hunt a predator, you gotta send in something just as dangerous."

I stood up. "I said no."

But he didn't blink.

"I never told you this," he continued, "but he emailed me last week. Burner account. Said he had information."

I froze. "About what?"

"Didn't say. Just said 'It's time you knew what's really happening.'"

I closed my eyes. The Professor.

The man who once mentored us. Trained us. Inspired us. Then betrayed us. Disappeared when things got too hot. Left Bronx bleeding and me spiritually cracked open.

Now he was back?

"Why would he help us?" I asked bitterly.

Bilal shrugged. "Maybe guilt. Maybe leverage. Or maybe he just wants to be in the mix again. Either way…"

"The timing is too close," I finished.

He nodded.

"I'll reach out," I said reluctantly. "But we don't give him anything. Not yet."

"Of course."

Bilal stood, handed me the bottle of zamzam, and walked toward the door. Just before stepping out, he paused.

"Jibril, you know what this is, right?"

"What?"

"This isn't just about finding her. This is about deciding what kind of man you're willing to become to do it."

That night, I didn't sleep.

Not even pretend-sleep. Not the tossing and turning kind, either. I sat in the prayer room long after 'Isha, knees stiff on the musalla, forehead against the carpet so long I lost track of time. My duas were messy—half Arabic, half broken English, all fear.

I didn't beg for miracles.

I begged for clarity.

I begged to still be worthy of the trust my daughter used to place in me. For her heart to remain whole. For Allah to protect her from anything I couldn't see—and everything I'd failed to prepare her for.

Sara came in quietly at one point, wrapped in her robe, eyes puffy from her own sleeplessness.

She didn't ask anything. Just sat beside me, leaned her head on my shoulder, and prayed silently.

After Witr, she placed her hand gently on my back. "Whatever it is," she whispered, "don't carry it alone."

But I already was.

The hardest thing about being a man in leadership isn't the pressure—it's the expectation that you never break. That you never sit in a room and say, I'm scared. That you never admit when the house is on fire and your heart is the first thing burning.

I thought I had learned balance.

But what I'd really learned… was suppression.

And Sakeena—God help me—she learned it too.

By morning, I was already halfway through my coffee when Bilal called.

"He wants to meet."

"Where?"

"Coffee shop in Austin. Neutral ground. One hour."

"Is it safe?"

He paused. "Not even a little."

But I was going.

Because fathers don't wait for safety.

They walk into danger with their hands open and their hearts broken.

Because the moment you become a parent, your life is no longer your own.

As I packed my bag, I stared at Sakeena's note again.

Please don't come looking for me.

But that's the thing about love.

We look anyway.

Even if it costs us everything.

Even if it means going back into the shadows we swore we'd never enter again.

Because I wasn't just going to find a daughter.

I was walking toward the man who taught me how to build a movement…

…and nearly taught me how to burn one down.

After Bilal left, I stayed in the apartment.

I don't know why.

There was nothing left to find—no hidden clues, no forgotten diary pages, no social media account left logged in. Just quiet. And dust. And the feeling of being too late.

I picked up her Qur'an from the dresser and flipped through it gently. There were soft pencil marks beside ayat about trust, justice, mercy. I found a sticky note near Surah Maryam—she'd written "beautiful and powerful, just like the women I needed around me."

I smiled. Then I broke.

Because how do you prepare your daughter to face the world without making her fear it?

How do you protect her without caging her?

How do you teach her to survive without hardening her heart?

I remembered one night—she must've been sixteen—when she came home from a school field trip early. I was on the porch reading, the air thick with the scent of jasmine and distant barbecue.

She dropped her backpack at the door and sat beside me.

"You ever feel like you don't belong anywhere?" she asked.

"All the time."

She didn't speak for a while. Then said, "I stood up for a girl on the bus. Her hijab got pulled off as a joke. Nobody cared."

"You did."

"Yeah. But then I got laughed at too. The teacher said I was being dramatic. One kid called me 'Taliban Barbie.'"

I clenched my fists even now remembering that.

She continued: "So I sat in the back. Quiet. Pretended like I didn't hear anything the rest of the ride."

"I'm sorry," I told her that night.

And I meant it.

She looked up at me with wet eyes. "I know you're busy trying to fix the world, Baba. But sometimes I just want you to fix mine."

That memory stabbed deeper now.

Because here I was again—busy trying to fix the world.

And I might have let hers fall apart.

I drove to Rasheeda's that night.

She met me outside, wrapped in a loose shawl, her hair uncovered. That was rare. It meant she was tired. Raw. Done pretending.

"She's been unraveling for months," she said as we sat on her porch. "I didn't want to say anything because I thought she'd figure it out. But I saw it—the sadness behind her smiles. The way she'd avoid eye contact anytime we talked about relationships, about faith, about trust."

"Why didn't you tell me?" I asked.

"Because I didn't want her to think we were conspiring. Because I was scared you'd try to fix it when what she needed was space."

I nodded slowly. "I gave her space."

"No," Rasheeda corrected gently. "You gave her distance."

That one landed.

We sat in silence for a while.

"She's not gone," Rasheeda whispered.

"I know."

"She's watching us. Waiting to see if we'll chase her or let her go."

I didn't respond.

Because I still didn't know the answer.

The next morning, I packed light.

A prayer rug. A notebook. A copy of The Autobiography of Malcolm X— my original one, spine cracked, full of margin notes from college. And the bottle of zamzam Bilal had left behind.

Sara didn't ask where I was going.

She just stood in the kitchen, pouring milk into Imani's cereal bowl, eyes on the spoon but heart in the doorway.

"You prayed on this?" she asked quietly.

"Every hour since yesterday."

She nodded. "Don't let the man you were meet the man you left behind."

I didn't know what that meant until I got in the car.

On the drive to Austin, I thought about him—The Professor.

The man who'd taught us how to organize, how to speak with our backs straight, how to outmaneuver the press and outquote the Qur'an in strategy meetings.

He was a storm in a three-piece suit. Muslim, brilliant, fearless. Too fearless. He taught us how to lead, but not how to pause. How to build momentum, but not how to brace for impact. He quoted Baldwin, Fanon, and the Sahabah all in the same breath.

He made us feel invincible.

Until the night he almost got us killed.

The night of the private fundraiser that turned into a raid.

The night Bronx ended up bleeding in an alley while we scattered like hunted men.

We never spoke again after that. He vanished.

Until now.

And I couldn't stop wondering why.

Why come back now?

Why through Bilal?

Why with secrets?

And most of all—

What did he know about my daughter?

The coffee shop was tucked in the corner of an East Austin plaza, gentrified but not yet entirely stolen. Murals of Black poets still clung to the walls like protest notes no one had the courage to erase. I parked in the far corner and waited. No sudden moves. No dramatic entrances.

Bilal pulled up ten minutes later and nodded at me through the windshield.

Then we walked in.

And there he was.

The Professor.

Older. Leaner. Wearing glasses this time, and a black kufi pulled low. He didn't rise to greet us. Just looked up and gestured to the seats across from him.

"Jibril," he said.

His voice was the same—smooth, slow, like he was always thinking three sentences ahead.

"Before we begin," he said, "I want you to know—I didn't come back for redemption."

Bilal looked at me.

I said nothing.

Because I already knew:

He came back for leverage.

And my daughter was the price.

Chapter Five

Coffee and Contradictions

I hadn't seen The Professor in almost a year.

And even then, the last time we were in the same room, Bronx was bleeding out on a sidewalk in South Houston, a cracked rib and a busted jaw the final punctuation to a plan gone sideways. I still remembered the look in his eyes—rage, betrayal, hurt. Not just from the injury, but from the realization that we were pawns in someone else's game.

Now here I was. Two hours from home, staring at a ceramic mug I didn't order, waiting on a man I once followed like a prophet.

The café was the kind of spot where revolutionaries didn't belong, but sometimes hid. Wood-paneled walls. Abstract art for sale. Indie jazz humming from overhead speakers. The chalkboard menu had more milk alternatives than prayer spaces. I scanned the room—mostly grad students and freelancers, lost in laptops, all unknowingly sharing oxygen with the ghost of a nearly-burned movement.

Bilal had stayed behind, parked across the street in a borrowed sedan. Said one of us needed to keep eyes from a distance. He'd wired me up with a discreet mic—a small dot tucked just beneath my collar. I'd called it overkill. He called it insurance. After everything we'd seen, I couldn't argue.

Then he walked in.

The Professor.

Like nothing had happened.

Salt-and-pepper beard, edges a bit less precise than I remembered. Same polished composure, but thinner now, like his presence had faded in places. He moved through the café like a man who didn't want to be remembered. Or maybe one who couldn't afford to be.

He sat across from me without a word. Nodded once. Took a slow sip of his espresso.

I noticed his hands trembled—subtle, but real.

"You lost weight," I said.

He smiled faintly. "You didn't bring Bronx."

"Didn't bring my boxing gloves either."

He chuckled—dry, humorless. "You still pray before you swing?"

"Only if I intend to land it."

There was a pause. That old tension returned like dust in the air. Heavy. Familiar. The kind of weight that doesn't ask permission to settle.

"I heard about the mall," he finally said. "Bronx handled himself well."

I didn't respond. I just stared at him—studying his posture, his carefully chosen words, the way he avoided direct eye contact for more than a few seconds.

The thing about men like him is they don't crumble. They recede.

"You didn't call me to talk about that," I said flatly. "What do you know?"

He exhaled through his nose, like even speaking cost him something. "I know your daughter's been asking questions. Poking around in things that aren't clean."

"Be specific."

"She accessed backup files. Financial records. Early communication threads between donors and founding members. I assume she got them off Sahara's laptop."

He took another sip. "I had digital tripwires on some of those folders—traces. Old habit."

My jaw tightened. "What kind of records?"

He looked me in the eye for the first time. "Enough to make you question the integrity of Black Up 2.0. Enough to confirm that some of your allies never left the plantation—just bought a new one."

I sat still. Silent.

"You ever wonder why your funding tripled this year?" he asked. "Why the board shifted tone but not skin tone?"

"I'm not naïve," I said.

"Then why are you surprised your daughter smelled the rot before you did?"

That landed.

Not because it was an insult—but because it was a truth I hadn't fully faced.

Sakeena had always seen through facades. Even as a child, she had a way of asking the question nobody wanted to answer. I remembered once, when she was twelve, she sat on my lap during a strategy meeting and whispered, "Why do the rich Muslims give money only when there's a camera?"

That moment haunted me then.

It haunted me more now.

"Where is she?" I asked, my voice low.

"I don't know," he said. "But I know who does."

He reached into his notebook and pulled out a folded napkin. Slid it across the table like a chess piece.

One name. Inked in neat block letters.

Rashad.

It hit like a ghost.

He was one of the original fundraisers—part of the old movement before we cleaned up the brand. Never in the front. Never on flyers. But always at meetings. Quiet. Always watching.

And when everything fell apart, he vanished.

I hadn't heard his name in over a year.

"Why would she go to him?" I asked.

The Professor leaned in. "Because she's trying to find out if Black Up is a movement—or a market."

The words stung.

Because they weren't just about her.

They were about all of us.

"I don't want her getting hurt," I said, trying to steady the tremble in my voice.

The Professor gave me a look that felt like both a mirror and a warning.

"Then stop trying to parent from a pedestal. She's not a pawn in your moral chess game. She's a grown woman with your fire in her veins—and maybe too much of it."

"I've tried to guide her."

He nodded. "But you never let her see you bleed."

That stopped me.

He kept going.

"You want her to see your leadership. But she also needs to see your fear. Your flaws. That's how legacy works—not through perfection, but through presence."

I clenched my fists under the table. "You lost your right to give counsel."

He didn't flinch. "And yet, you still came to see me."

I stood. "Give me the last known address."

He scribbled something on the back of a business card and slid it across the table.

As I reached for it, he said, "Don't let your anger drive the car, Jibril. Or you'll crash into your own reflection."

I looked at him one last time. And for a brief second, I didn't see a mentor or a traitor. I saw a man who once believed so hard in justice that he forgot to check the cost of the methods he used.

"You don't tear down a house while people are still living in it," I said.

Then I walked out.

Bilal was in the car, engine running, eyes fixed on the door.

"Well?" he asked.

"He gave me a name. Rashad."

His jaw tensed. "That brother's a ghost. Thought he dipped overseas."

"Apparently ghosts leave trails," I said, holding up the card. "And my daughter followed one."

He glanced at it, then nodded slowly. "So what's the play?"

"We find him. Then we find her."

I didn't say the rest out loud—but it rang loud in my mind:

We were standing at a crossroads. Between power and principle. Between movement and manipulation. Between protecting our people and performing for them.

And my daughter was already walking ahead of us on that path.

Rashad.

That name brought more than memories—it brought shadows.

He was never flashy. Never loud. While we stood on stages and passed the mic, he stayed in the back. Quiet. Eyes always scanning. He wasn't the one taking the photo—he was the one making sure the photographer had a waiver on file.

He handled logistics. Spreadsheets. Permits. The donors. Especially the donors.

When we were younger, it felt like a relief to have someone like that. Someone who could "deal with the money folks" while we stayed in the trenches.

But then things shifted.

I remembered the first time I questioned him. We were prepping for the launch of a youth mentorship campaign—Black Up's first national project. I was in the office late, reviewing numbers. Rashad had left his laptop open. I saw donor names we weren't supposed to have.

Names from corporations we'd openly criticized.

Names from community developers with gentrification lawsuits still pending.

"Where's this money coming from?" I asked him later.

"Where it needs to come from," he said coolly. "You want results or righteousness?"

That should've been the day I pulled the plug.

Instead, I let it slide. Told myself we'd clean it up later. That the mission justified the mess.

That was the beginning of the unraveling.

I sat with that memory in silence as we pulled away from the café.

Bilal didn't say anything for a few minutes. Just drove, hands tight on the wheel, eyes on the road.

"You believe him?" he asked finally.

"Enough to be scared."

He nodded. "Same."

The city blurred past our windows—billboards, mosque domes, Black-owned food trucks, protest flyers stapled to telephone poles. I saw everything. I felt none of it.

"I hate that we're here," I said.

"Yeah."

"I hate that our movement was supposed to free our kids… and now mine's running from it."

"She's not running from it," Bilal said, glancing at me. "She's interrogating it. And maybe that's what we raised her to do."

That made my throat tighten.

I looked down at the napkin with Rashad's last known info. I didn't recognize the address. Some rural zip code outside San Antonio. Quiet. Off-grid.

"Ghost town," Bilal muttered.

"We'll find him," I said. "Then we find her."

"You still think she's with him?"

"No," I said. "I think she went to him for answers."

"Which means she knows more than we do."

And that was the real fear.

That my daughter was three steps ahead of us—and we were only now realizing we'd left the map behind.

That night, back home, I sat alone in the living room with the lights off.

Everyone was asleep—Sara upstairs with the twins, Imani curled on the couch in her favorite blanket fort, a half-eaten apple beside her. The silence was thick. Sacred. And heavy.

I thought of Sakeena.

Perhaps, I never had a good answer to all of her tough questions.

Maybe that's why she went searching.

Maybe she got tired of watching people pray like warriors, then lead like politicians.

Maybe she needed to know if the fire we carried was real—or just smoke for photo ops and fundraising.

I opened my notebook.

Not the movement binder. Not the strategy journal. My real one. The one with du'as, confessions, sketches of ideas I was too afraid to say out loud.

I flipped to the last page and wrote:

If she exposes what we buried…

Is that still betrayal?

Or just accountability from the next generation?

The next morning, Bilal texted me before sunrise.

"Address confirms. Rashad lives off-grid. Tiny cabin outside La Vernia. You ready?"

I typed back: "As I'll ever be."

Then I sat at the edge of the bed.

Sara stirred. "Another trip?"

I nodded.

"You bringing armor or humility?"

That question lingered as I packed my bag.

Because the truth was—I didn't know which one would save me.

And I had a feeling I'd need both.

Chapter Six

Ghosts Don't Bleed

The address on the napkin led us through a forgotten edge of Houston—where streetlamps flickered like dying stars and sidewalks cracked like old bones. It wasn't far from an industrial district we used to canvas during food drives. But this wasn't charity territory anymore. This was silence-and-surveillance territory. The kind of place where people went to disappear, and no one asked questions if they didn't return.

We turned off the main road and coasted down a half-paved lane, gravel popping beneath the tires like gunfire in slow motion. A single warehouse loomed ahead—tin walls, no signage, just a steel door and one crooked light barely clinging to its post.

Bilal scanned the area for the third time in two minutes. "You sure this isn't a setup?"

I stared through the windshield. "If it is, it's a pretty low-budget one."

"Don't get cute. You didn't see what happened to Kareem."

I didn't respond. I didn't want to think about Kareem. I didn't want to think about any of the brothers we'd lost to burnout, breakdowns, or worse. Not tonight.

We parked a block away, behind a hollowed-out taco stand that hadn't sold anything but rumors in years. The smell of grease and stale beer still clung to the walls like a memory no one asked for.

Bilal adjusted the strap across his chest.

"You brought heat?"

"Always," he said, without looking at me. "Especially when ghosts start calling meetings."

I wasn't armed. I told myself it was a conscious decision—peace over paranoia. But deep down, I knew it was pride. I didn't want to admit I was afraid.

We stepped out into the night, boots crunching glass as we crossed the broken sidewalk. The air was thick. Warm. Still. The kind of night that felt like it was holding its breath.

We didn't speak as we approached the warehouse.

The side door was half-cracked, paint peeling like a bad secret. Bilal paused to listen. Then he nodded. We slipped inside.

The inside of the warehouse smelled like mildew and metal. Dust floated in the air like pollen from a dead season. Our boots echoed with each step across the concrete floor, the sound bouncing off the walls like a warning we hadn't earned.

I moved slow, careful, trying to push down the flood of memories now rising inside me. Because I'd been in places like this before. Meetings held in half-renovated buildings. Fundraisers that doubled as vetting operations. Basements where we whispered plans louder than we ever should have.

And Rashad?

He was always there.

Never the loudest voice. Never the one grabbing the mic or leading the du'a. But always close. Always in the loop. Always in the room.

I used to call him "the ghost of the movement." Half joke, half warning.

There were signs, of course.

The whispered jokes about him playing both sides. The time someone caught him in a private meeting with a state rep we had publicly condemned. The moment he redirected a major donation—$25,000 from an anonymous "foundation" that nobody could verify.

"Trust him," I told Bilal back then. "He's a chess player, not a street preacher. We need both."

Bilal didn't argue. But I remember his face that night—tight jaw, slow nod, a silence I hadn't learned to fear yet.

Another brother, Kareem, had been more direct.

"You're building something righteous," he told me. "Don't hire men who profit off shadows to guard the door."

But I did.

Because Rashad got results.

Because the money flowed when he made calls.

Because our school doors stayed open and our food pantries stayed full.

Because sometimes when you're starving to build something, you stop reading the fine print on the hand that's feeding you.

Now here I was, back in a space he had chosen, wondering what it would cost this time.

A shuffle echoed through the corridor.

Then footsteps—quick, familiar.

"Sakeena!" I hissed, trying to keep my voice controlled.

Silence.

Then, from the shadows: "Dad?"

I turned the corner fast, heart pounding.

There she was.

Hood up. Backpack strapped tight across her chest. Shoes scuffed. Eyes sharp and wide like someone caught halfway between fight and flight. She looked thinner. Paler. But not broken.

She wasn't a victim. She was a storm mid-formation.

"You okay?" I stepped forward, arm halfway out.

She took a small step back—not fearful, just… distant.

"I'm fine," she said. Two words that carried too much.

Bilal stood behind me, posture quiet but locked. One hand near his jacket, the other hanging low, fingers loose like a switch was waiting to flip.

"Sis," he nodded, eyes scanning her for injuries, threats, signs.

"Bilal." Her voice was clipped. She gave him a nod that landed somewhere between caution and contempt.

No hugs. No tears. Just three people standing in the middle of dust and distrust.

"You didn't think I'd come," I said.

"No," she replied flatly. "Not here."

"Why not?"

"Because this place—this part of what you built—it's not who you said you were. I hoped it wasn't."

She glanced around the warehouse like it was a mausoleum. Her face didn't carry fear. It carried disappointment.

The kind that hits harder than anger.

"You think I knew about this?" I asked gently.

She raised an eyebrow. "I think you didn't ask."

That one cracked something in me.

"You think I sent Rashad into hiding?"

"No," she said. "I think you didn't realize how many men like him you let move in silence."

There it was.

The accusation beneath the heartbreak. The truth beneath her retreat.

She hadn't run away because she was afraid.

She'd stepped back because she didn't like the version of me she was starting to see.

I looked at her. Really looked.

And for the first time in a long time—I didn't see my daughter.

I saw a mirror.

She led us deeper into the warehouse—past busted office chairs, filing cabinets with no drawers, a long-forgotten fax machine still blinking in permanent error. The air grew colder. Or maybe that was just my chest tightening.

At the far end, a single desk lamp cast a halo of yellow across a wooden table. Behind it sat a man who had once managed millions with a quiet smile and an even quieter soul.

"Rashad," I said.

He didn't flinch. Didn't rise. Just looked up from a small stack of paper and grinned.

"Jibril. Been a while."

That voice hadn't changed. Smooth. Polished. Laced with condescension even when wrapped in courtesy.

He hadn't aged much. Same sharp jawline, same tailored jacket—even here, in a warehouse. His posture said comfortable, but his eyes said armed.

"What is this?" I asked.

He nodded at a flash drive on the desk. "This is your inheritance."

"I didn't come for riddles."

He leaned back and crossed one leg over the other, relaxed in a way that made me itch. "You built a new house on the bones of the old one. And never once asked who cleaned up the mess."

"I shut down the old movement."

"No," he corrected. "You stepped off the stage. The script kept running."

Bilal stepped forward, hand hovering near his side. "You threatening him?"

Rashad raised both hands mockingly. "I'm just delivering mail. The envelope doesn't choose the message."

Bilal reached for the drive.

Rashad laid his hand flat on top of it.

"Uh uh. That's for her."

He nodded toward Sakeena.

"She asked the right questions. She gets the real answers."

I turned to her. My voice softened. "What's he talking about?"

She looked down, then met my eyes.

"Dad… there are accounts. Bank accounts. Shell corporations tied to nonprofits that are technically still active. Some of them funnel donations through foreign entities. Others trace back to private prisons and security contractors. The donors? They've got blood on their ledgers."

My jaw locked. "How do you know this?"

"I traced them. The registry names. The offshore branches. Sahara had a copy of the data. I just followed the trail."

My stomach turned.

Rashad finally pulled his hand away.

"You always wanted to save your people," he said. "But you let snakes finance the ladder."

I stepped closer. "You were part of it too."

"I was the snake," he said, almost proudly. "The difference is—I never lied about it."

The silence was dense. The only sound was the low hum of the desk lamp and the soft tap of Sakeena's fingers on the flash drive now resting in her hoodie pocket.

"What's on there?" I asked Rashad, my voice more gravel than tone.

"Everything you didn't want to know," he said. "Emails. Board votes. Donor roll calls. Strategic memos. Names of people you've hugged who were laundering the very oppression you preach against."

I clenched my fists. "You let this happen."

He didn't blink. "I orchestrated it. Because idealism doesn't pay rent. You wanted to open schools and fund clinics. I got the checks cut. You asked for impact—I delivered outcomes."

"At what cost?" I growled.

He shrugged. "The same cost every revolution pays: compromise."

Sakeena stepped forward. Her voice was low, but clear. "One of the shell nonprofits links to a firm that provides detention software for ICE. Another was a shell corporation with ties to a lobbying group that fought to keep military aid flowing to anti-Muslim regimes."

I turned to her, breath catching. "You're sure?"

"I triple-checked."

Bilal let out a low whistle. "That's not just messy. That's rotten."

Rashad smiled like a man who had been waiting for the truth to land ugly. "You built something beautiful," he said to me. "But the roots are soaked in someone else's blood. And now your daughter's holding the shovel."

I looked at her. Really looked. She wasn't afraid. She was resolved. And in that moment, I wasn't staring at my child.

I was staring at my successor.

"You planning to release it?" I asked.

She hesitated. Then said, "Not yet. But if we don't clean this up from the inside… I will."

Bilal muttered, "That would nuke the whole movement."

Sakeena didn't flinch. "Then maybe it deserves to burn."

I turned away. My throat was dry. My chest tight.

We had spent a decade building a house with faith and sweat.

And now we were learning the bricks were funded by betrayal.

"What are you going to do with it?" I asked her.

My voice cracked slightly, but I didn't care. This wasn't about strength. Not anymore.

She looked down, then back up. Her jaw was tight, her eyes dry. "I don't know yet."

"That's not good enough."

"I'm not trying to be good anymore, Baba."

She said it with steel. Not bitterness. Not defiance. Just… finality. Like she'd already buried the girl who used to beg for bedtime stories and folded her faith into a sword.

I stepped closer. "You think we sat on lies? You think we didn't fight for something better?"

"I think you fought the battles that made sense to you. The ones that didn't ask you to sacrifice too much. The ones that didn't force you to set fire to the people you once broke bread with."

I stared at her, stunned.

"Don't act like I don't know how this works," she continued. "You built a righteous brand. You held brothers accountable for their tone in sermons. You protested textbooks. You fought gentrification. But when it came to money? You looked away."

"That's not fair," I said.

"It's accurate."

I wanted to yell. To shake her. To tell her that she didn't understand the trade-offs. That survival sometimes comes before purity. That a movement isn't built in a vacuum. That nothing we did was ever simple.

But she already knew that.

And still, she chose truth.

Even if it meant burning everything.

"I made mistakes," I said, my voice low.

She nodded. "So did I. But I'm not going to keep making yours."

The silence that followed was worse than shouting. Because it wasn't war. It was departure.

I looked at Bilal. He looked like he wanted to speak. Wanted to tell her to pause. To weigh the long game.

But he didn't.

He just nodded slightly.

"She's not a kid anymore."

And he was right.

I had raised her to be brave.

Now she was.

Bilal hadn't moved much during the exchange.

But I knew him well enough to read the small things—the twitch in his jaw, the tightening of his stance, the way his left thumb kept brushing against the inside of his palm like a man holding back a fire.

Rashad leaned back in his chair, arms folded across his chest like he was watching a performance he'd seen before. Too calm. Too smug.

"You got something to say, brother?" he asked Bilal.

That word—brother—felt like an insult coming from his mouth.

Bilal didn't speak.

He just walked forward, slowly, until he was inches from Rashad's desk.

"You ever come near her again," he said, voice low, "I won't need a flash drive to erase you."

Rashad smirked. "Still the soldier, huh? I always respected your loyalty. Even when it blinded you."

"I'm not blind anymore," Bilal growled. "I see exactly what you are."

"A middleman?"

"A virus."

Sakeena put a hand gently on Bilal's forearm.

"It's not worth it," she said.

Bilal's shoulders dropped just slightly. He stepped back, shaking his head.

"I used to wonder how you slept at night," he muttered. "Now I realize—men like you don't sleep. You just reset your mask."

Rashad didn't reply. His silence wasn't surrender. It was strategy.

The kind of silence that waits for you to forget.

I'd seen it before—in courtrooms, in boardrooms, even on the masjid shura. Men like Rashad didn't panic when they were exposed.

They just pivoted.

We left without another word.

No handshake. No goodbye. No moment of closure.

Sakeena walked several paces ahead of us, her steps sure, her shoulders squared. She didn't look back—not at Rashad, not at me. She moved like a woman done waiting for permission.

The warehouse door clanged shut behind us, and the air outside felt even heavier than when we'd arrived.

Bilal walked beside me in silence.

We passed the busted taco stand, its faded sign flapping in the wind like a flag from a country that no longer existed.

I wanted to say something—anything—to lighten the weight pressing on my chest. But all I could think about was how long I'd ignored the warning signs. How many small compromises I'd filed under "necessary." How many backdoor deals I'd let slide because they came with a donation big enough to sponsor scholarships or rebuild gym floors.

And how my daughter—my fire-eyed, truth-telling, righteous daughter— had found the very skeletons I buried under budget reports and board meeting minutes.

"She's different," I finally said.

Bilal nodded. "Yeah. She's you. With better timing."

We reached the car.

Sakeena didn't wait for the front seat. She climbed into the back like a passenger, not a daughter. Like someone who knew she was part of the mission—but not yet part of the team.

As Bilal started the engine, I glanced at her through the rearview mirror.

She was staring out the window.

Expression unreadable.

Flash drive zipped into her hoodie pocket like a live wire no one wanted to touch.

"You believe her?" I asked quietly.

Bilal shifted into gear. "Does it matter?"

"Yeah. It does."

He pulled onto the road and let the silence sit a while.

Then finally: "She believes it. And that's enough."

That night, I couldn't sleep.

I lay in bed staring at the ceiling fan as it spun like time—slow, loud, unchanging. Sara stirred once, murmured something soft in her sleep, and pulled the blanket closer. I envied her peace.

In the next room, Sakeena was curled on a guest mattress.

Under my roof.

But not in my reach.

I heard her cough once. A small sound. Human. And it broke me more than any confrontation ever could.

I had spent years preparing speeches for stages, but now I couldn't find the words to reach my own daughter.

I sat up.

Reached for my notebook.

Wrote the only thing that made sense:

The truth is heavier when it comes from someone you raised to carry it.

I closed the journal and walked downstairs to the prayer room. No light.

Just me, the rug, and the long list of names I now whispered to Allah like a man asking forgiveness for sins he didn't even know he'd committed at the time.

I prayed for guidance.

For protection.

For the courage to let go of my version of the truth if hers proved closer to God.

Because righteousness without humility becomes tyranny.

And I had no interest in leading a movement if it meant losing the one person who reminded me why I started it in the first place.

Upstairs, I could still hear the faint rhythm of her breath behind a closed door.

Sakeena.

My mirror.

My reckoning.

My future.

And somewhere inside her hoodie, pressed against her heart—

—sat a flash drive that could tear everything I built apart.

Chapter Seven

Guns, Flash Drives and Baby Formula

"You ever get the feeling your daughter might be smarter than you?" I asked Bilal as we sat in the parking lot of a halal waffle house, staring at the sunrise like two unlicensed therapists on a cigarette break.

Bilal didn't blink. "My daughter's three, so not yet. But give her a couple more years. She already knows how to manipulate my wife, so the writing's on the wall."

The windows were fogged from the heat of our breath against the early morning chill. We hadn't spoken much since the warehouse. Not about Rashad. Not about the flash drive.

Not about the reality that my own daughter might have just uncovered enough dirt to bury the very foundation we built our lives on.

"I didn't think I raised a revolutionary," I muttered.

"You didn't," Bilal said.

He took a slow sip from a travel mug he'd refilled twice already.

"You raised a woman. And women are just revolutions in better shoes." I cracked a smile, then sighed. "She's got this way of looking at me now.

Like I'm… historic. Like I belong in a textbook she's already tired of reading."

"Join the club," Bilal said. "My wife calls me 'beloved' when she's mad. That's how I know I'm an outdated institution."

We sat for a while in silence. The kind that only happens when two men have seen too much, said too little, and understand each other without needing permission.

"You think I messed up?" I asked.

Bilal didn't answer immediately.

"I think we all did. Some of us just got better PR."

I stared out the window.

"I was so proud when we got the first grant. Remember that? Five figures from that interfaith justice collective in Maryland. I remember holding the check like it was divine revelation."

"And then we spent it in three days feeding the entire Southside during Ramadan," Bilal said. "That was real. No one's questioning that."

"But we never asked where the next check came from."

"No," he said, finally turning to look at me. "We asked. We just didn't wait for the answer."

That one cut deep.

He was right.

Because somewhere along the way, I stopped reading the fine print.

And now my daughter had read every last clause.

When I got home, the house was already pulsing with noise.

One twin was screaming like someone told him the milk was haram, and the other was dangling half-asleep in Sara's arms, his pacifier hanging on for dear life. The living room looked like a toy grenade had gone off—blankets, burp cloths, bottles, and something sticky I chose not to identify. Sara didn't look up from her station on the couch.

"How'd it go?" she asked, bouncing gently as she bottle-fed the quieter twin.

"You ever try reasoning with someone holding your secrets on a USB stick the size of a thumb drive?"

"Did you say thank you?"

"For what?"

"For not uploading it to Instagram with a Drake quote under it."

I exhaled a tired laugh and took the louder twin from the playpen before his vocal cords filed a lawsuit.

I bounced him on my shoulder while checking the stove. Cold. Leftovers from last night untouched. The TV was playing reruns of a cooking competition that none of us had watched past the intro, but the volume helped drown the sense that the world was tilting.

"She called me," Sara said casually.

I turned, already bracing.

"While you were in the shower. Said she was sorry. Said she's not trying to go rogue. Just… trying to understand how things got so tangled."

"She said that?"

"She also asked if we ever considered restarting the organization under a new name, new board, new funding source, full transparency."

I raised an eyebrow. "Did she also propose a zakat audit committee and a Qur'anic compliance review board?"

"Actually, yes."

I stopped bouncing the baby for a second.

"You laughing at me or praying for me?"

She smirked. "Can't I do both?"

The baby spit up on my shirt mid-chuckle.

Right on cue.

As I changed into a fresh hoodie, I glanced at a photo on the wall—one I hadn't really looked at in a long time. It was from Sakeena's eighth-grade debate tournament. Her in a navy blue hijab, fists curled in excitement, standing on the stage beside a boy twice her size that she'd verbally dismantled over the ethics of drone strikes.

I remember that day like it was an ayah I never forgot.

She had stood in the middle of a white auditorium, mic trembling in her hand, and said, "The problem with American policy is that it trains its allies like dogs, then acts surprised when they bite."

Afterward, I'd asked her where she got that line.

She said, "You. You said it last Ramadan during a halaqah."

I hadn't even remembered saying it.

But she remembered everything.

She had always been listening.

Later that week, we gathered at Rasheeda's house.

It smelled like cardamom and deflection—something warm and nurturing that barely masked the tension bubbling underneath. She'd made lamb stew with cornbread and a side of sweet mint tea. Comfort food. The kind of meal that made you want to confess… or cry.

Bronx answered the door wearing house slippers and a neck pillow, his certification results clutched like a diploma.

"I swear if this meeting's about more problems, I'm walking out. I just got my final results and I'm finally certified to teach gym, math, or fight off generational trauma."

I clapped his shoulder. "Relax. You're not in trouble. Yet."

He gave me a side-eye, then nodded at Bilal. "You bring drama?"

Bilal shrugged. "Just the usual brand."

We prayed together in Rasheeda's den—soft carpet, window light cutting through sheer curtains. Then we sat in a wide circle, tea in hand, plates half-full, eyes wary.

I dropped the bomb gently. "Sakeena's got something."

Everyone froze.

Bronx's fork stopped mid-air.

Rasheeda lowered her tea like she suddenly remembered it might be poisoned.

"She's got what?" Bronx asked, setting his plate down.

"Receipts," I said. "The financial kind. From the old movement. Donors we never vetted. Money tied to some names we don't want to be associated with."

"Define don't want to," Rasheeda said sharply.

"Think oil tycoons who fund prisons and anti-Muslim lobbying arms," Bilal said.

Bronx whistled. "You're telling me we got blessed by devils?"

"Basically."

A long silence settled like steam over the table.

"What's she planning to do?" Rasheeda asked.

"She hasn't said," I replied. "She's thinking. Processing."

"That's code for prepping a press release," Bronx muttered.

Bilal leaned forward, elbows on knees. "We could go public. Get ahead of it. Issue a statement, launch a full financial review, rebuild the movement from the inside out."

"Or," Rasheeda cut in, "we tell her to pause. Remind her there's still value in protecting a house while it's being cleaned. You don't burn down a mosque just because someone miscounted the donation box."

"But if the foundation's compromised…" Bronx began.

"That's the question," I said. "Is this movement reformable—or has it been rotting under our feet while we ran PR campaigns and community programs?"

Rasheeda looked at me long and hard. "Is this your daughter's revolution… or your guilt speaking through her?"

I didn't answer.

Because I wasn't sure.

It was late.

The house was finally quiet—twins asleep, the hum of the fridge playing background music to my anxiety. I found Sakeena in the kitchen, barefoot in leggings and one of Sara's oversized hoodies, staring into the open fridge like it owed her answers.

She looked like she hadn't slept in days.

"Want something?" I asked.

"Yeah," she said without turning. "Clarity."

I leaned against the doorway. "That's in the cabinet under the snacks. Right next to the regret."

She smiled, but it didn't reach her eyes.

We stood in silence for a minute.

Then: "You mad at me?"

"No."

"Disappointed?"

"Not in you."

She finally turned. Her face was softer in the low light, but her eyes were still firm.

"I wasn't trying to blow it up. Not at first."

"I know."

"I just couldn't unsee what I saw. Once I found that folder… once I saw where some of the money came from…"

"You felt betrayed."

She nodded slowly. "I wanted to believe the movement was clean. Or at least… cleaner than the system it fights."

I sighed and sat at the table. "We did our best, Sakeena."

"I know you did."

She poured herself a glass of water, then sat across from me.

"But doing your best and doing what's right… they don't always land in the same place."

That one hurt.

Because she said it gently. Like she was trying not to break me.

"You think I failed?"

"No," she said. "I think you succeeded at something… and now we're all figuring out what it really cost."

I looked at my daughter—this woman I helped raise on bedtime surahs and protest signs—and for the first time in years, I realized I couldn't protect her from the truth.

She had outgrown the myth of me.

And now she was choosing whether to burn what I built—or rebuild it without me.

Sunday brunch rolled around like clockwork.

We gathered at the spot on Heights—high ceilings, halal everything, and just enough grease in the grits to remind you of your grandma's kitchen. The kind of place where men wore kufis with sweatsuits, and arguments about theology were settled with sweet tea refills.

Abdul arrived first, draped in a bomber jacket with a Malcolm X pin that looked like it had been through the revolution itself.

"Who's leading today?" he asked, sliding into the booth. "If it's another lecture on fatherhood, I'm leaving. My kid just told me I'm too 'snacky' to be taken seriously."

Isa showed up next—Gap hoodie zipped to his chin, Quran app already open on his phone like it was armor. Revert brothers always came prepared. Ameen, our quiet ex-Marine turned imam-in-training, followed. He didn't say much—he never did—but the way he listened could humble a whole panel of scholars.

I laid the issue out clean. No sugar. No spin.

"Let's say, hypothetically," I began, "someone finds out that the movement we built was, at some point, funded by sources that—if exposed—could delegitimize everything we've done. What's the move?"

Abdul raised his hand like he was in Sunday school. "Burn it all and start over."

Isa shook his head. "Not so fast. You make a public statement. Name what you knew, when you knew it. Take accountability. Then shift all donations into a transparent, third-party-reviewed trust."

"And if people ask why we didn't vet our donors?" I asked.

"Tell the truth," Ameen said quietly. "Say you were too busy feeding people to realize who was paying for the plates."

Abdul leaned back. "Or say nothing. Stay silent. Let the next generation fix it."

"Or," Isa added, "be the next generation yourselves and fix it now."

There was a pause.

Then I asked the question I hadn't said out loud until now.

"What if the truth destroys us?"

Abdul didn't hesitate. "Then maybe we weren't as solid as we thought."

That night, the house was quiet again—but I wasn't.

I sat at the dining table long after everyone had gone to bed. The kitchen light above me buzzed faintly. The rest of the house felt like it was holding its breath.

In front of me sat my laptop.

Beside it: the flash drive.

Small. Harmless-looking. Just plastic and metal.

But in my chest, it throbbed like a live grenade.

I picked it up, felt its weight—more symbolic than physical—and rolled it between my fingers. Sara passed by quietly, her hair wrapped, a cup of warm tea in her hands.

"You still haven't looked at it?" she asked softly.

"Part of me wants to pretend it doesn't exist."

She nodded. "But?"

"But the other part already knows it does."

She placed her hand on my shoulder. "Allah judges you by your intentions."

"I know."

"But the IRS judges you by your receipts."

I stared at her.

"You comforting me or scaring me?"

"Yes," she said, and walked off without looking back.

I plugged the drive in.

The screen blinked.

A folder opened.

Inside—dozens of files.

PDFs. Screenshots. Scanned checks. Emails. Meeting minutes. Account summaries.

All organized. Annotated.

Timestamped.

Names I knew. Foundations I'd partnered with. Anonymous donors whose "generosity" I had once thanked publicly on stage.

One email chain showed a grant—$80,000—from a security consulting firm that had lobbied for predictive policing software. Another outlined a donor board meeting where a proposal passed to filter movement money through a shell nonprofit registered to an address in the Caymans.

The worst?

A scanned note from a former adviser confirming that we should avoid "overly ethnic branding" in Black Up's second-phase marketing campaign.

To "not alienate moderate allies."

I closed the lid.

Sat there.

Alone.

Breathing shallow.

This wasn't just uncomfortable.

It was unholy.

The movement I helped build—the one with Qur'anic mission statements and interfaith partnerships and polished youth programs—had been partially funded by mechanisms of the same system we were trying to dismantle.

Sakeena hadn't overreacted.

She'd restrained herself.

I stood up, walked to the window, and stared out into the night.

Streetlights.

Silence.

The weight of a future I no longer owned.

Tomorrow, we'd have to decide how much of this to reveal.

And to whom.

But tonight?

Tonight I just let myself feel it—

The truth.

Heavy.

Burning.

Chapter Eight

Shadows on the Perimeter

The morning felt… off.

Not chaotic. Not loud. Just wrong.

The birds outside the window weren't chirping like usual. The sky was gray, not storm-gray—just undecided, like it hadn't made up its mind about the day. Even the neighborhood kids who usually raced their bikes past my driveway were missing. The silence wasn't peaceful. It was staged.

And Sara?

She was on her third cup of tea by 8:00 a.m.

Not coffee—tea.

That was her tell. Tea meant worry. Tea meant thinking. Tea meant something's not right but I'm not ready to say it out loud yet.

I was sitting on the edge of the bed, watching one of the twins sleep in the bassinet and pretending I hadn't been awake most of the night. I kept checking my phone out of habit. Notifications, group texts, random emails—but nothing urgent. Just an unsettling stillness.

Then it rang. Bilal.

Not a text. A call. And Bilal never called. He was a voice-note kind of guy.

A three-word reply kind of guy. But this—this was a call.

I answered, still groggy. "As-salaamu Alaikum—"

"Can we meet? Now."

My spine straightened. "You okay?"

"No." His voice was tight. Tired. "Bring Bronx. You'll want backup."

Click.

No du'a. No details. Just dread.

I stood up slowly, the room spinning a little with the weight of that last word.

Backup.

That's when I knew—whatever was coming, we were past the point of quiet conversations.

Something had shifted.

And we were already behind.

We met in an abandoned church on the edge of the city, just past the tracks where the streetlights get scarce and the buildings start looking like broken teeth.

It wasn't our usual kind of spot.

Too exposed to feel safe, too forgotten to feel secure.

But it had history.

Black Up used to hold tutoring sessions here when we were just getting started—back before donors, before hashtags, before mission statements with legal disclaimers. Just mismatched chairs, dry-erase boards that barely worked, and young Black boys sitting cross-legged on the floor asking questions about the Qur'an, algebra, and America in the same breath.

We eventually outgrew the space.

Or maybe we told ourselves that to mask what really happened: that we became too polished to keep returning to places that didn't have functioning bathrooms or air conditioning.

That church was dust now.

Dust and echo.

Bronx met me out front, a hoodie over his cornrows and a cautious squint in his eyes. He looked like he hadn't slept either.

"You know what this is?" he asked me quietly.

"No," I said. "But Bilal said bring backup."

Bronx raised an eyebrow. "Well, I brought faith and a blade. Hope one of them works."

We walked in through a side entrance with a busted lock, past cracked tile and rusted pews. The stained-glass windows were mostly intact, casting strange, fractured rainbows across the floor.

Bilal was already inside.

He stood near the front, behind a fold-out table he must've dragged from the storage closet. A manila envelope in one hand.

A pistol in the other.

"Is this a sermon or a crime?" Bronx asked, eyes narrowing.

"Depends," Bilal muttered.

He didn't look up. Just laid the pistol down with care and slapped the envelope on the table. His eyes were bloodshot. His beard a little more grown than usual. And his posture—worn. Like he'd been carrying too much for too long and was finally letting his back acknowledge it.

"Talk to us," I said.

"Someone's been following me."

"Us?" I asked.

He nodded. "Not metaphorically. I mean, black car. Tinted windows. No plates."

"You sure?" Bronx asked, shifting his stance.

Bilal reached into the envelope, pulled out a photo, and tossed it on the table.

Grainy. But undeniable.

A figure in a dark jacket, face turned slightly, caught mid-step near one of our newer school buildings.

"Rashad?" I asked.

Bilal shook his head. "No. Worse."

I didn't ask who.

Because my gut already knew.

This wasn't just about betrayal.

This was surveillance.

This was war.

The church air was thick with dust and memory. I stared at the grainy photo, trying to match it with anything from our past—but the face was too obscured. Still, my body remembered what my mind couldn't quite name.

This wasn't new.

It was just finally undeniable.

I leaned against the pulpit—the same one we used to stand behind when reading Qur'an aloud for the young boys from the neighborhood. Now I was leaning against it like a man confessing instead of teaching.

"You remember that forum we did at the city rec center three years ago?" I asked Bilal.

He nodded slowly. "The prison-to-school pipeline one?"

"Yeah. Two nights after that event, I saw a white van parked outside my house. Didn't think much of it. But it was there again the next morning. Then again later that week."

"I remember," Bronx said. "Didn't we joke about it being the feds?"

"We did," I said. "We laughed. We prayed. Then we stopped mentioning it."

Bilal exhaled through his nose. "Because we thought being Black and Muslim and bold was enough armor."

"Because we thought we weren't important enough to watch."

The silence that followed was heavy. Not the awkward kind. The kind that confirms a fear everyone had been privately nursing.

"There were signs," Bronx added. "That youth retreat we canceled after that donor pulled out? He didn't pull out. He was advised to distance. He told me off the record."

"Advised by who?" I asked.

Bronx looked down. "He didn't say."

Bilal rubbed his temples. "So we've been targets. We just didn't realize we'd moved from 'potential' to 'priority.'"

I paced the space where the front pews used to be. "We thought we could out-organize scrutiny. That if we stayed righteous enough, prayed long enough, served hard enough, we'd be safe."

Bronx scoffed. "Ain't no such thing as safe when you're trying to wake up a system that profits from your sleep."

We all stood there, surrounded by what we used to believe in—now peeling off the walls like old paint.

And I realized: this wasn't just a threat.

It was a reminder.

They'd been watching.

We were just late to look back.

Later that night, I called the only kind of meeting I trusted anymore.

No livestreams. No press releases. No folded arms in a circle of twenty men quoting Malcolm but hiding ego behind every "As-salaamu Alaikum."

Just four people.

Me.

Bronx.

Bilal.

And my daughter.

Yeah, I invited Sakeena into a situation that might kill us. I knew that. I also knew she was the only one brave—or reckless—enough to ask the questions that made everyone else squirm.

We met in Bilal's garage.

No overhead lights. Just a bare bulb dangling from a wire like a witness.

Sakeena walked in with that same laptop bag over her shoulder, hoodie zipped to her chin. Her hair was tied back, her eyes sharper than I'd ever seen. She looked like a defense attorney crossed with a digital activist. Calm. Intentional. Unapologetic.

"You sure about this?" Bilal asked her.

She didn't blink. "I wasn't raised to be quiet in the face of injustice."

Then she turned to me.

"That was you, remember?"

Touché. Again.

She plugged in the flash drive and turned her screen so we could see. Rows of folders. Code-named, timestamped, but clean. She clicked one.

Wire transfers. A dozen of them.

Accounts we didn't recognize. Names we hadn't approved.

She pointed to a highlighted section. "It's not just where the money came from. It's who helped move it."

Bilal leaned forward, the lines in his forehead deepening. "You mean…"

"Someone on our board. Maybe two."

She clicked again—another folder. Email chains, anonymized contracts, signed digital forms.

"See this? This LLC? It's fake. But it was used to launder nearly $140,000 from three donors who have direct ties to private detention centers and military surveillance firms."

Bronx let out a long whistle.

"Names?" I asked, already bracing.

"Not yet. But I'm close," she said. "I'm just tracing the signatures and metadata."

"You learned all this on your own?"

She didn't answer.

That was answer enough.

Bilal backed away from the table and ran a hand over his face. "She's not just uncovering problems. She's walking us into a war."

"Then maybe it's time we stop pretending we're still in peacetime," Sakeena said.

I stared at her.

At my daughter.

And I saw the future—not the one I planned, but the one I earned.

A future that no longer needed my permission to arrive.

The next morning, I was half-awake and mid-dua when my phone buzzed like it owed someone money.

Isa.

Not a call I was expecting. Not this early.

His text was brief. Too brief.

"Brother Jibril, we need to talk. It's urgent. Don't bring anyone."

I stared at it for a full minute. Thought about ignoring it. Thought about deleting it. Thought about texting Bilal and telling him I was being set up. But I didn't.

Because that's the problem with trust—you don't realize it's fractured until you start checking who's behind every message.

I drove to the masjid on the east side. We met at a bench just behind the wudu station—one of those quiet spots where conversations get swallowed by the rustle of trees and the hum of old air vents.

Isa was already there, sitting stiffly, wearing sunglasses that felt like a costume.

"Trying out for the FBI?" I asked as I sat down.

He didn't laugh.

"I got a call last night," he said.

"From who?"

"I don't know. They didn't say a name. Just that they knew who I was, and that they knew what I was involved in. And that if I valued my future, I'd stop helping you."

My jaw tightened. "What exactly are you helping me with?"

He didn't answer right away. Just stared into the distance like he was watching a future fade.

"I don't know, Jibril," he finally said. "But you need to hear this. This movement… it's not just about us anymore. There are people watching. And not just the ones you expect. Some of them are closer than you think."

"That a warning?"

"That's a promise."

His tone didn't change. He didn't blink. He wasn't scared—but he wasn't comfortable either.

I looked at him hard.

"You believe in what we're doing?"

"I did."

"Do you now?"

"I believe in truth. And I believe the closer you get to it, the more likely someone is to put a price on your head."

We sat in silence after that.

I left that meeting not sure if I'd just spoken to a friend—or to my Judas.

When I got home, Bronx was already in the garage.

Sweat dripping.

Knuckles bruised.

Punching the heavy bag like it owed him child support and gas money.

Each thud echoed off the cement walls like a warning shot.

"You good?" I asked, leaning in the doorway.

He didn't stop. Just muttered between swings, "Just prepping."

"For what?"

He paused. Let the bag swing, hands on his knees, breath thick.

"I don't know," he said. "But something's coming. And I don't want to be soft when it does."

I nodded, because I felt the same.

Like we were training for a battle we hadn't named yet. Like something under our feet was about to crack open and swallow what was left of the movement whole.

Inside, Sara was in the nursery.

One twin on her hip, half-asleep. The other wailing from the swing like the world was ending and no one told him what time.

She looked up when I stepped in, then looked back down, bouncing gently, whispering whatever incantations mothers use to silence apocalypse in infant form.

"You know what scares me more than the threats?" she asked, not lifting her eyes.

"What?"

"That you might stop fighting because it gets too dangerous."

I didn't say anything.

Because there was no good answer.

"I won't stop," I said, finally.

"Even if it costs you your life?"

"That's not the plan."

She gave me the wife look. The one that said plans don't mean protection.

"Legacy means nothing," she whispered, "if it leaves us with graves instead of guidance."

That stayed with me.

Long after the twins quieted.

Long after she fell asleep.

I stood by the crib that night, watching two little boys dream beneath soft lights and chaos, wondering if they'd inherit a movement—or just the ashes of one.

That weekend, we met again.

No livestream. No agenda. No tea or snacks.

Just storm clouds and suspicion.

The five of us—me, Bronx, Bilal, Sakeena, and Isa—gathered in the basement of the old community center. The walls still carried faint graffiti from teenage rebellion: phrases like "We all we got" and "Build or be buried."

The lights flickered. The storm overhead cracked like a whip every few minutes.

Perfect ambiance for a confession… or a collapse.

Sakeena stood near the center, laptop open, flash drive already plugged in. She didn't wait for ceremony.

"I've traced the donor chain," she began, scrolling. "There's a middleman—someone running a fake LLC that funneled large donations from sources we should've never touched. One of those names is a firm connected to private defense contractors. Another links to a fund that backed anti-Muslim political ads in the last two election cycles."

She tapped the trackpad, opened a PDF, and slid a printed document across the table.

"Guess who signed off on the funding protocol?"

We all leaned in.

A name.

Not just familiar. Trusted.

Bronx sucked air through his teeth. "No way…"

Bilal muttered a dua under his breath. "I should've known."

I stared at the signature, unable to reconcile it with the man I'd prayed beside, strategized with, wept with in janazahs.

Sakeena wasn't done. "He's tied to Rashad. There are email threads. Encrypted, but I cracked a few headers. There's chatter about 'damage control' and 'minimizing Jibril's reach.' There's even a line about—" she hesitated "—'disposing of Sakeena if necessary.'"

My stomach flipped.

Bronx stood, fist clenched. "He dies tonight."

"No," I said, standing too. "Not yet. We're not that kind of movement."

"Maybe we should be," Bilal said. His voice was steady. His eyes weren't.

Then I noticed Isa.

Silent.

Still.

Watching the document too long.

Not enough surprise in his face.

Too much calculation.

"You know something?" I asked him.

He shook his head too quickly. "I'm just here to help."

That was the moment.

I didn't know who the traitor was.

But I knew someone wasn't going to make it out of this clean.

And someone—maybe more than one—was already marked.

Outside, thunder rolled again.

And in that basement, five of us stood in silence, each one wondering if the war had already begun—

—and if the first casualty was going to be trust.

Chapter Nine

Smoke Before Fire

They say the hardest part of being a man isn't providing.

It's pretending everything's fine when your world's buckling beneath your feet, and somehow still managing to show up for carpool duty and salat like you're not quietly spiraling on the inside.

That week, I became a black belt in pretending.

I went to work. I returned calls. I even made small talk with the neighbor who insists on giving unsolicited parenting advice while her own toddler throws rocks at our mailbox. I nodded politely, waved back, and clenched my jaw so tight my molars held a protest.

I mowed the lawn. Twice. Which wouldn't be weird except it had rained both times, and we don't even have grass in half the yard. Sara didn't say anything about it, but she did watch me from the kitchen window like I was either preparing for judgment day or mid-nervous breakdown.

She never pushes. That's not her style.

She's the kind of woman who folds socks like she's praying over them. Who clears dishes with the silence of a woman choosing peace over performance. But she notices everything.

The way I sat a little too still during Qur'an recitation.

The way I stared too long at the boys' baby monitor, like I was waiting for it to short-circuit and take me with it.

The way I opened the fridge and closed it three times without taking anything out—because sometimes even decision fatigue starts in the dairy section.

Finally, one morning over breakfast, she looked up from her tea and said, "You're moving funny."

I blinked. "Funny how?"

"Like a man waiting for a bomb to go off."

I chewed my toast like it had suddenly betrayed me. "I don't know what you mean."

She raised an eyebrow. "Exactly."

That's when I knew I wasn't hiding anything. I was just making it harder for her to help.

Because the truth was, I felt like a man sitting in the center of a circle made of glass. Every conversation. Every meeting. Every text message I reread four times before deleting.

All of it was weight.

And at some point, something had to crack.

Friday evening found us in the side room at the masjid.

Not the main prayer hall, not the multipurpose room with folding chairs and that one cousin who always "accidentally" breaks the mic. No, this was the dusty side room with a flickering fluorescent light and a bookshelf full of outdated Islamic studies textbooks no one dared throw away.

Bilal had claimed the spot like a man preparing for judgment—or court.

He stood by a half-broken table, one foot tapping steadily like his pulse was trying to keep the beat. Bronx leaned back in a chair with one leg folded under him, sipping from a styrofoam cup that smelled like it came from the masjid's basement vending machine. Possibly expired.

Isa was already seated. Hoodie zipped. Arms folded. Quiet.

Me? I brought coffee. It felt like a defense mechanism at this point.

Bilal didn't waste time.

"We're being followed."

I looked up, mid-sip. "Again?"

"Again," he said flatly, dropping a black envelope on the table like it contained divorce papers from Allah Himself.

He pulled out grainy photos. One of him stepping into his building. Another of Bronx and me leaving brunch last week. And one that made my heart skip: a shot of my driveway from across the street.

"This ain't paranoia," Bronx said. "This is calculated."

"Exactly," I added. "Calculated people don't show their hands unless they're sure of the outcome. So what do they want?"

Isa finally leaned forward, speaking slow. "They want to discredit us. The movement. You especially."

"Why now?" I asked.

He glanced toward the window, like someone might be listening. "Because it's growing again. Not loud, not flashy. But steady. Quiet movements make powerful enemies."

Bilal rubbed his beard. "And powerful enemies don't issue warnings. They send messages."

"Or silencers," Bronx muttered.

Nobody laughed.

We sat in that stuffy room with bad lighting and old books, trying to solve a mystery that felt more personal than political.

I looked around the table.

A fighter. A planner. A silent skeptic. And a man who felt like he was holding it all together with tape, prayer, and outdated passwords.

"We need to know who's leaking," Bilal said.

I nodded, but inside, something else was stirring.

What if the leak wasn't an outsider?

What if it was already in the room?

When I got home that night, the house was dim and soft and suspiciously peaceful.

Which in our household meant someone was either asleep, plotting, or emotionally preparing a conversation.

I found Rasheeda in the living room sitting cross-legged on the floor with Imani. They were counting prayer beads. Imani was narrating each count like she was delivering a khutbah for the stuffed animals lined along the couch.

"And then you say Subhan'Allah again, even if you forgot, because Allah still knows, and you might get extra points just for trying."

Rasheeda chuckled. "That's actually better theology than most YouTube da'wah bros."

I cleared my throat at the doorway. "Why does she always come to you with this stuff?"

"Because I listen better," she said without looking up.

I stared at her.

"You could've kept that to yourself."

She shrugged, still smiling, still counting beads with Imani. "She says your face looks tired. Like your eyes are arguing with your mouth."

I wasn't sure if I was offended or seen.

I stepped inside and sat on the edge of the couch, leaning back like it could hold more than just my spine.

"Been a long week," I muttered.

"You said that last week," she replied.

I nodded. "And it was true then, too."

Imani ran upstairs to fetch her "dua notebook," leaving Rasheeda and me alone in that comfortable, judgment-free, sarcasm-filled kind of silence we'd mastered over the years.

"She's worried about you," Rasheeda finally said.

"Sara?"

"Her too."

She handed me a fresh cup of tea. Jasmine. Always jasmine when things felt heavy.

Then, with no fanfare, no raised voice, she dropped it:

"You trust Isa?"

Simple. Direct.

A grenade under the table wrapped in lace.

I didn't respond immediately. Sipped the tea. Too hot. Still drank it.

"I trust that he's useful," I said.

She raised one eyebrow—the Rasheeda Special.

"And you trust that's enough?"

"I trust that Allah sees all."

"Fair," she said. "But you might want to start seeing a bit more yourself. Before someone sees it for you."

I looked at her. Really looked.

And in that moment, I remembered why women lead movements in everything but title.

Because they ask the questions the rest of us avoid.

And they don't need a stage to do it.

The next afternoon I met Bronx at the gym.

We were both dressed like we intended to lift something heavy, but all we really lifted was accountability and doubt.

The locker room smelled like chalk, effort, and a little too much Axe body spray.

We sat on the bench, side by side, staring at the weight racks like they owed us answers. Other brothers moved through the room—some nodding in recognition, some too deep in headphones to notice anything but the beat.

We weren't there to train.

We were there to breathe without explaining ourselves.

"You ever think we're in over our heads?" I asked.

Bronx didn't flinch. He wiped his forehead with a towel, though we hadn't even broken a sweat.

"You're just now asking that?" he said, grinning. "Bro, I thought it was obvious when we almost got locked up over a mall food court brawl and still followed it up with a press release and a prayer circle."

I laughed louder than I meant to.

"Look," he said, "we didn't sign up to be saviors. We saw something broken and tried to fix it. That's all."

I nodded. "Yeah. But the fixing feels heavier now."

"Because it is."

Bronx stretched his legs and leaned back. "This ain't the beginning anymore. In the beginning, it was us and flyers and late-night group chats.

Now it's donations, security cameras, missing money, and board votes. This is grown-man revolution. You feel it in your knees."

"Speak for yourself," I smirked. "My knees gave up two leadership retreats ago."

He chuckled, then grew quiet.

"You think Isa's clean?"

I didn't answer right away.

"I think… I don't know. But that's part of the problem. I used to know. Used to be sure."

Bronx nodded. "The moment you stop knowing who you can trust, that's when it stops being a movement and starts becoming a minefield."

I stared at the floor tiles. "You still in?"

"Always."

"Even if this gets ugly?"

He looked at me. Same brother who once fasted for seven days to support a protest, who buried his cousin from gun violence on a Friday and still taught a youth class that Sunday.

"Ugly's never stopped me before."

That night, I couldn't sleep.

It wasn't fear. Not in the classic sense. No shadows lurking in the hallway. No nightmares.

It was something quieter. Sharper.

Anticipation.

The kind that buzzes beneath your skin. The kind that whispers that something is about to happen—but not what, or when, or where. Just soon. That ambiguous, suffocating soon.

I sat on the edge of the bed, scrolling through old emails, rereading donation memos I once skimmed like they were harmless. Noticing patterns. Repeated names. "Consulting firms" that didn't exist on Google. Timestamped receipts that didn't match the events we held.

The Professor had gone quiet again. No strange emails. No midnight messages from unknown accounts. But his silence was louder than any warning.

Isa was being too helpful. Too consistent. Offering resources we hadn't asked for. Showing up early to meetings like he was campaigning for sainthood.

And Sahara? Sahara had been calling more often.

She'd leave voicemails at odd hours. Always the same concern: "Just checking in on Sakeena. Let me know if she needs anything."

Which would've sounded kind—if her timing didn't align with every major move we made.

The pattern was tight.

Too tight.

I got up, made wudu, prayed two rak'ah for clarity. No lightning bolts. No divine download. Just a lingering sense that we were running out of time.

So I did what I hadn't done in months:

I called a full meeting of the brothers.

No agenda.

No bullet points.

Just a time, a location, and a menu.

Sunday morning. Pancakes. Grits. Chicken sausage.

We would speak.

And I would stop holding the weight alone.

The brothers came hungry.

That was always the trick.

You could get men to show up for a 7:00 a.m. Quran circle maybe once a month—but throw in grits, pancakes, halal sausage, and bottomless coffee? They'd beat the sunrise.

The brunch spot was buzzing. Same long wooden table in the back, same peeling mural of Malcolm and Muhammad Ali dap-fisting over sweet tea, same uncle who always overcooked the turkey bacon and asked about your marriage whether you were married or not.

It wasn't everyone. Some were traveling. A few had fallen off over the past year—new jobs, new wives, or maybe just too many wounds from the last implosion.

But the ones who came?

They were listening.

Isa was there, seated with his back to the wall like he didn't trust anyone behind him. Abdul showed up in a kufi and Timberlands like he was prepared for either prayer or protest. Even young Amin came, quiet and eager, clutching a journal like he was ready to take notes for a revolution he hadn't yet seen.

I didn't have a speech.

Didn't need one.

I let the food settle. Let the chatter calm. Let the brothers feel human before I reminded them what was at stake.

Then I stood.

"I don't have all the details," I said. "But I know something's off."

Heads turned. Forks paused.

"There are people watching us. People we thought we left behind. People we thought were gone."

Silence.

I kept going.

"Some of it's surveillance. Some of it's internal. Maybe even in this room."

A few eyes flickered. No one moved.

"But this isn't just about one person. This is about all of us. The movement. The vision. Our families. Our schools. Our intentions."

I paused. Let that land.

"They want this to fall apart. Not with guns. With doubt. With scandal. With distraction. They want us to self-destruct."

Abdul cleared his throat and stood. "We knew this day would come. The day the work became a threat. The question is… what do we do now?"

The brothers looked at me.

And I looked back at all of them.

I saw fear. Yes. But I also saw tired loyalty. Unspoken bonds. That brotherhood forged in late-night cleanup duty, tear-filled janazahs, and making tahajjud in school gymnasiums while janitors swept around us.

"We do what we've always done," I said. "One step. One prayer. One community event at a time."

It wasn't fire and fury.

It wasn't a rallying cry.

But it was a pulse.

And it reminded us: we were still alive.

Still choosing this.

Even if it burned. Even if it broke us.

Because movements don't die from bullets.

They die from silence.

And we were done being quiet.

Chapter Ten

A Cold Wind at Sunrise

A Cold Wind at Sunrise, delving into Jibril's sunrise anxiety, his spiritual fragmentation, and the subtle dread hovering over ordinary life. Tone: reflective, atmospheric, slightly humorous in weary moments.

Mornings in Houston had their own kind of silence.

Not the kind that kissed your soul, like the opening credits of a retreat video. This was the kind of silence that crept in like fog and sat on your chest. Like the city knew something you didn't. Like the wind had been told to hush before delivering bad news.

I woke before Fajr, no alarm needed. Just my body jolting into awareness like a soldier trained for tension. There was no sound. No dreams left behind. Just that thick quiet and a lingering ache in my ribs that wasn't physical.

I lay there for a while, staring at the ceiling fan spinning like it was chasing something it could never catch. Sara stirred next to me, her breathing slow and even. Peaceful. I envied that.

"You okay?" she mumbled, her voice wrapped in sleep.

"I will be," I said.

It wasn't a lie. It was a prayer disguised as confidence.

I slid out of bed, moving carefully so the mattress wouldn't groan. I padded into the hallway and peeked into the twins' room. Both were still—one with a foot sticking out from under a blanket like he was testing the weather. The other curled into a half-moon of innocence.

I smiled despite the weight in my chest.

Then I stood still for a long moment, hand on the doorframe, waiting for something I couldn't name.

Sometimes the body knows when life is about to tilt. Your breath shortens. Your hands go restless. Your thoughts start running drills.

I made wudu in the dark, letting the cold water snap me into clarity. Each splash felt like a countdown.

The drive to the masjid was quiet. The roads looked asleep. Streetlights blinked in sync like they were meditating. Every red light felt longer than usual, like time itself was pausing to see if I'd turn back.

I didn't.

When I arrived, I was the second car in the lot.

The first belonged to an older brother named Idris—retired, widowed, and faithful like clockwork. He prayed Fajr at the masjid every day without fail. Said it helped him "remember that time was short, but purpose was long."

I entered the prayer hall and breathed in the scent of aging carpet, oud, and yesterday's hopes. The brothers trickled in slowly, sleep still clinging to their eyes, some in work boots, some in thawbs, all with that unspoken understanding that dawn prayer was more than ritual—it was armor.

We prayed.

We rose.

But no one left.

That was the first sign something was off.

Usually, the brothers scattered like seeds in the wind after Fajr—work shifts, morning runs, rushed commutes. But this morning? They lingered. Some sipped coffee from dented thermoses. Some stared out the stained-glass windows. The air was charged, like the masjid had been holding its breath.

Even Ameer—the brother who always made a joke about something, anything—was uncharacteristically quiet. Just sitting with his hands clasped, eyes distant, like he knew the punchline but had lost the will to tell it.

"You ever get the feeling we're on the edge of something?" I asked no one in particular.

The question hung in the air.

Abdul finally responded, his voice calm and ancient. "We're always on the edge, Jibril. The question is whether we fall or fly."

Cryptic. Classic Abdul.

I let the words sit with me as I stepped outside.

The sun hadn't broken the horizon yet, but the cold wind did.

And it carried a warning.

The café Bilal picked wasn't one of our usual haunts.

It was tucked between a laundromat and a thrift store, barely wide enough to seat ten people. Ethiopian-owned. No sign out front—just a faded coffee cup decal on the window and a handwritten note that read, cash only, no nonsense.

Inside, the air smelled of roasted beans and burnt patience.

Bilal was already at a table in the back, black kufi tilted, sunglasses still on like he was auditioning for a spy film with a tight budget. He looked sharper than usual—white tailored thobe, pressed sleeves, tasbeeh in one hand, and a quiet storm brewing behind his calm.

"Got your text," he said as I slid into the seat across from him.

He placed his phone on the table, screen down.

I mirrored the motion without thinking.

"What's going on?" he asked.

"I think something's up with Isa."

Bilal didn't blink. Just tilted his head slightly, like a man who'd already solved the riddle and was just waiting to see if you'd catch up.

"You just figuring that out?"

I clenched my jaw. "He's been avoiding calls. Said he was traveling for family stuff but never gave details. Bronx said he spotted him two days ago. Downtown. Alone. Near city hall. Didn't look casual."

Bilal finally removed his glasses, folded them slow. "I've been watching him."

That gave me pause.

"You've been what?"

"Nothing serious. Just patterns. Time stamps. Presence versus absence. The way he started volunteering more right after the Rashad files showed up. The way he always brings solutions we didn't ask for—then disappears."

He took a sip of tea and grimaced. "Still bitter."

"The tea?" I asked.

"The betrayal," he said. "But yeah, the tea too."

We both exhaled.

"I wanted to believe he was sincere," I said, quieter this time.

"Wanting don't make it true."

There was history behind those words.

Bilal had trusted a brother once. Years back. When Black Up was barely a whisper of an idea. That man had taken $30,000 from our early donor fund and "vanished" on a dawah tour to South Africa. We found out later he used it to buy property in Georgia.

Bilal never spoke that brother's name again.

"You think Isa's working alone?" I asked.

"No one this smooth works alone," he replied. "He's either a pawn or a plant. The real question is: does he even know which?"

Our food came—injera, lentils, spicy beef. We barely touched it.

"I'm tired," I admitted.

"Then stretch, not quit."

"That easy?"

"No. That necessary."

We sat in that silence for a long time. The kind of quiet where strategy starts to form—not in plans, but in permission. Permission to question everything. Even each other.

Outside, the wind kept pressing against the windows like it was trying to warn us.

Something was coming.

We just didn't know from where.

Back home, the day moved slower than it should have.

The light in the living room was too soft. The hum of the fridge too loud.

Even the twins were quieter—napping longer than usual, as if the whole house had decided to hold its breath.

Sara was in the dining room setting up for her revert sisters' Zoom session. She had her notebook open, tea steeping beside her laptop, and that half-concentrated expression she wore when she was about to carry other people's burdens while hiding her own.

I stood in the doorway longer than I meant to.

She didn't look up.

"You ever feel like your heart knows something before your mind is ready to accept it?" I asked.

She paused.

"Only every other Tuesday," she said softly.

That made me chuckle, but only for a second.

She turned in her chair to face me.

"What is it?"

"I think I lost a friend."

She didn't ask who. Sara never needed details to offer comfort. She just needed truth.

"Someone you trusted?" she asked.

I nodded.

"Someone you defended?"

"Publicly. Privately. At meetings. In the masjid parking lot. You name it."

She exhaled. "That's the worst kind."

"What is?"

"The kind of grief that doesn't get a funeral. Just silence."

I walked over and sat next to her. "I keep trying to make excuses for him. That maybe he's under pressure, maybe he's scared, maybe—"

"Maybe he made a choice."

Those four words hit harder than any lecture.

Because she was right.

There's betrayal. And then there's disillusionment. One comes with drama and flames. The other shows up slow, wearing your friend's voice and your shared memories like a disguise.

"I thought we were building something sacred," I whispered.

"We still are," she said. "But sacred doesn't mean safe."

I stared at her. At the woman who'd been holding me up longer than I cared to admit. At the woman who never asked to be part of this movement but had sacrificed more than most who had.

"You ever regret signing up for this life?" I asked.

Sara tilted her head. "I didn't sign up. I fell in love. Then I stayed."

I leaned forward, elbows on knees, trying to gather strength from a conversation that felt too honest.

"What if the damage is already done?"

She rested her hand on my back, firm and warm.

"Then you rebuild. Brick by brick. With the people still standing."

The email came at 5:42 p.m.

Subject line: URGENT—Review This Now

The sender? A brother from the community board. A cautious man. One of the few who never bought into hype, conspiracy, or Twitter scholarship. If he was forwarding something with all caps in the subject line, it was serious.

I opened the link.

A PDF report. Government letterhead.

Preliminary Findings: Suspected Subversive Activity – Internal Memo (Restricted)

My chest tightened.

Right there in the middle of the third paragraph:

"The following grassroots organizations are being monitored for financial inconsistencies, unregistered foreign donations, and ideological indicators of extremism…"

Then a list.

Ten names.

Ours was second.

Black Up Movement (Greater Houston Area)

I kept reading. Audit procedures. Freezing assets. "Potential risk assessments" for board members. Community centers. Youth programs. All flagged.

At the bottom, in smaller print, one line that lit my blood on fire:

Source: Confidential legal consultant (internal affiliation: Black Up)

Sara stood behind me, reading over my shoulder.

I didn't hear her enter. But I felt her breath catch.

"You trusted him," she whispered.

"I know."

That was all I could say. My mouth had forgotten how to form complete thoughts.

The room went cold.

Not because the temperature changed. But because everything we had built—every speech, every fundraiser, every youth session—was now part of a federal file.

The phone rang.

Then another.

Then three more.

My WhatsApp exploded. The brothers were already talking. Screenshots were circulating. Voice notes flying back and forth.

One brother texted:

"Did you know?"

Another:

"What do we tell the youth?"

Another:

"Are we safe?"

And that last question?

That was the one that cracked something open inside me.

Because I didn't know anymore.

At the masjid office that night, it was chaos.

Brothers pacing in corners. Sisters crying quietly in the hallway. Ameer trying to calm everyone down with jokes that landed like bricks.

Bronx showed up in all black, hoodie up, face hard. He didn't say much— just stood next to me like a wall with fists.

Bilal had his laptop open, already scanning documents, comparing language, highlighting inconsistencies.

"The leak came from inside," he confirmed. "Isa gave them everything. Donation trails. Meeting minutes. Old draft proposals we thought we deleted."

"How do you know?" I asked.

"He signed the access logs."

Silence.

Abdul sank into a chair and just muttered, "Astaghfirullah" over and over again.

"We trusted him," I said.

"We let him in," Bronx added. "And now the community's bleeding for it."

I didn't argue.

Because they were both right.

That night, I didn't sleep.

Sleep felt optional. Prayer didn't.

I made wudu slow, deliberately. Like maybe if I washed my limbs long enough, I could rinse the betrayal from my chest too. The water was cold, and I didn't flinch. I welcomed it. Let it remind me that I was still here. Still flesh. Still fighting.

I prayed like I hadn't in years.

Not the kind of prayer you perform. The kind you survive.

There were no eloquent duas. No polished Arabic. Just a cracked voice, a tight throat, and a prayer rug that knew more of my grief than most of my friends.

I prayed for the youth who looked up to us.

For the elders who defended us at dinner tables they were barely invited to.

For the wives who stood beside us while we stood in front of bullets—metaphorical and otherwise.

For the brothers who bled truth but had no bandages for the aftermath.

And then, finally, for Isa.

Not out of forgiveness. But out of fear. Because I had seen what betrayal did to the soul—and I wouldn't wish that hunger on anyone.

I stayed in sujood until my back ached.

And still I stayed.

Because it wasn't just guilt or fear.

It was mourning.

For what we lost.

For what we might still lose.

And for the version of myself I had to bury in order to lead the version that must now rise.

Somewhere in the stillness, between tasbih and tears, I heard it.

A voice I hadn't invited, but couldn't escape.

The Professor's voice.

Smooth. Inevitable.

"Revolutions don't ask for permission."

I opened my eyes, my forehead still pressed to the earth.

"No," I whispered.

"But they pay in blood."

Chapter Eleven

Shadows and Spotlights

There's a kind of peace that feels earned.

And then there's the kind of peace that feels like the universe is winding up for a punch.

That's the one I had.

Life had started to fall into something that resembled a rhythm again. Not a symphony—more like a jazz set with no clear melody, just vibes, and occasional loud cymbal crashes in the form of toddler tantrums and surprise bank notifications. But it worked.

The boys were finally sleeping in longer stretches. One of them had even started pointing to the prayer mat when I said "Allahu Akbar," which made my heart swell and my eyes mist up like I was watching a Disney dad redemption arc.

Imani had learned how to spell her name out loud, slow and proud, like she was auditioning for spelling bee greatness one syllable at a time.

"I-M-A-N-I!" she shouted from the bathroom one morning, toothbrush still in her mouth. "That's ME!"

I almost cried brushing my teeth.

Sara and I had figured out a kind of groove. Not romance-novel smooth. More like Netflix-series married. We'd go from deep conversations to silent standoffs, from "you're my best friend" to "move your charger cord off my side of the bed" in under ten minutes. And somehow that felt… solid. Like grown love.

Rasheeda had taken charge of weekend story circles for sisters at the masjid, mixing tafsir with Toni Morrison quotes and almond chai. Bronx was mentoring again. Even Bilal had stopped randomly pacing like he was waiting for a coup.

We were healing.

Kind of.

Sahara was still quiet. Since the funeral, she'd been more shadow than presence. Her smile was always delayed—like it had to check in with a memory first before showing up.

I didn't push.

Grief moves like molasses in winter. Slow. Sticky. Cold.

And besides, for the first time in months, nobody was calling in panic. The group chat was full of memes instead of missing persons reports. Bronx even sent a selfie with one of his mentees, captioned: "Lil man said he wanna grow up and be a Muslim with muscles. I told him I'm both. He said 'Nah, I meant muscles for real.'"

I laughed harder than I should've.

For about three weeks, life resembled normal.

Until it didn't.

Until peace reminded us what it really was: the dress rehearsal before chaos.

It came on a Thursday.

I remember because Thursday is the one day I try to check out early—log off work, ignore texts, catch up on dua, maybe even walk barefoot in the backyard and pretend I understand grounding. But that Thursday? No peace.

It started with a ping.

Isa sent it. No message. Just an image.

A digital flyer. Cream background. Elegant serif font. A stock photo of a city skyline blurred just enough to hide which one. And right in the middle:

"Strategic Muslim Organizing in Urban America"

Guest Lecturer: Professor Mahmoud

Sponsored by the Center for Modern Faith and Civic Engagement

I stared at it for a full minute before my eyes remembered how to blink.

No slogan. No footnote explaining where he'd been. Just the man's name.

The Professor.

Suited. Trimmed beard. Polished glasses. Arms crossed in authority.

A full-blown academic brand.

I'd seen that posture before. I'd stood beside it when he told us we were the ones chosen to change the narrative. I'd seen it in a dusty office with dry-erase boards filled with arrows, fire, and prophecy.

Now he was in a press release.

"Modern Faith," I muttered aloud. "This dude was quoting Malcolm and threatening to boycott fried chicken spots with Zionist owners—now he's partnering with sociologists and policy interns?"

Sara peeked over my shoulder. "Is that…?"

"Yeah."

"Is he…?"

"He is."

She exhaled sharply, handed me my tea, and walked away without another word.

I stared at the screen again.

Underneath the event title, it described him as a "Community Strategist and Conflict Resolution Specialist."

I nearly choked on the tea. Conflict resolution?

This man once squared up with two board members over whether zakat funds could be used for bulletproof whiteboards.

This man told a grieving mother to "sacrifice comfort for the cause" when she asked for counseling after her son's arrest.

And now he was holding a mic on a university stage?

The comments online were already lit with praise:

"So glad to see him back."

"He's always been a visionary."

"The real ones never stay silent for long."

I wanted to scream. Or throw the phone. Or maybe just scroll into oblivion.

Instead, I called Bronx.

He picked up on the first ring.

"You saw it?" I asked.

"Oh, I saw it."

I waited.

"He's like a vampire," Bronx said, his voice calm but charged. "Just when the garlic wears off, he comes back with a suit and a slideshow."

I laughed, because it was true.

And terrifying.

We called it an emergency meeting, but there were no panic alarms.

Just text threads that moved fast. GPS pings that tracked cars to the masjid parking lot. A quiet understanding that sometimes, when the past circles back, you don't wait until Sunday brunch.

You gather your people.

The masjid multipurpose room was still half set up for youth night—folding chairs scattered, a half-deflated basketball in the corner, and a dry-erase board with a forgotten message that read: "Stay Woke, Stay Wudu'd."

Bronx was the first to arrive. Hoodie, joggers, and a knuckle bruise that said he'd been training hard.

Bilal followed, already on his second black coffee of the day. His eyes carried the weight of someone who'd read the fine print—and the footnotes—and still wasn't sure he'd gotten the truth.

Isa showed up last, laptop in hand, face tight. He'd taken the flyer personally. It wasn't just an old ghost returning; it was the man who nearly destroyed our momentum now being elevated as a model.

We sat around the table like old generals, staring at a laminated flyer like it held war plans.

"This is more than an event," Bilal said, setting his phone face down. "This is a narrative play. He's not just speaking—he's rewriting history."

Bronx nodded. "He gets credibility on that stage, it's only a matter of time before someone hands him funding, space, and a team."

"And just like that," Isa added, "he's back at the table—this time wearing a scarf instead of a fist."

We were all quiet for a moment.

Because it wasn't fear holding our tongues. It was something worse: the possibility that people might believe him.

Not the people in the trenches with us. Not the families who lost their sons. But the new ones. The young professionals. The nonprofits. The ones who only knew the surface. Who wanted movements that looked good on PowerPoint.

"He's going to bury the truth," I said finally. "Gloss over the missteps. Frame it all as passion mismanaged instead of betrayal well executed."

"So what do we do?" Bilal asked.

I leaned forward.

"We speak."

"Where?" Bronx asked. "You want to show up to the university and interrupt him like we're protest kids from the '60s?"

"No," I said. "We make our own event. Same weekend. Same topic. Different tone."

Isa raised an eyebrow. "You're serious?"

"Dead serious. We title it 'The Real Work.' No frills. No spectacle. Just voices that lived through it. Women. Youth. Elders. The brothers. Even that imam who almost shut us out during the fallout—I want him there too."

Silence again—but this time it was thoughtful. Calculating.

Bronx finally grinned. "You want a counterpunch."

"No," I said. "I want truth to walk onstage with no makeup and say: 'This is what happened, and we're still here.'"

The energy in the room shifted.

We weren't defending.

We were reclaiming.

We moved fast.

Bronx started with the title.

The Real Work: From Tragedy to Transformation

Simple. Sharp. Not too academic. Not too street. Just true.

Bilal called it "unapologetically unpolished." Isa said it sounded like a documentary. I said it sounded like something people could trust—and that was what mattered.

We locked in the venue: a community center in Third Ward that used to be a jazz club before gentrification swallowed the soul from the block. Now it served as a catchall for weddings, food drives, and occasional spoken word nights that leaned heavy on heartbreak and halal smoothies.

We set the date—same weekend as the Professor's lecture. Not to overshadow. To offer something different.

Then we got to work.

Rasheeda reached out to two local youth poets. Bronx called the families of former students. I tapped a sister who'd organized food security drives during the hurricane cleanup last year. Isa volunteered to run tech and graphics—he was still rebuilding trust, but this helped.

Ameer came up with the flyer design. Just black text on a white background. No logos. No sponsors. Just a silhouette of a clenched fist holding a Qur'an.

Raw. Quietly militant. Perfect.

We posted it on Friday night.

By Saturday morning, my phone had thirty-seven unread messages.

By Sunday afternoon, we had three hundred RSVPs—and a waitlist.

Something was moving.

Something was humming beneath the surface.

The people weren't just ready. They were starving for something real.

I got DMs from folks we hadn't heard from in months.

"I've been waiting for y'all to speak."

"Finally, someone said it out loud."

"Count me in. I'll bring my whole MSA."

Even one of the sisters who used to critique our flyers for "too much testosterone energy" said she wanted front-row seats.

The city was bracing.

And for once, we weren't reacting.

We were setting the terms.

The Professor's event had seats left.

Ours had standing room only.

And still, I didn't trust the silence.

The silence didn't last.

A few nights before the event, Isa called me late—later than usual, and Isa was already a 2 a.m. text kind of brother.

"You sitting down?" he asked.

"Not anymore," I said, standing up in reflex, already pacing toward the kitchen like the fridge held answers.

He hesitated.

"I got wind of something."

I waited.

"There's a proposal being floated. Quietly. No media. No public record. Just… whispers."

"From who?"

"Old donors. Some of the ones we cut ties with."

My grip on the phone tightened. "And?"

"They're shopping a new initiative. Community infrastructure. Education hubs. Civic engagement. All the right language."

I closed my eyes. "And let me guess—guess who's listed as the lead advisor?"

"Professor Mahmoud. Of course."

I exhaled. The kind of exhale that didn't relieve anything—just made room for more rage.

"They're rebuilding the original blueprint," Isa said. "But this time, with cleaner language, better marketing, and no messy idealists in the way."

"They're trying to make him the face again."

"And if we don't stop it," he continued, "he won't just rewrite the past. He'll design the future."

I was quiet.

Not because I didn't have a response—but because my response wasn't clean. It was full of curse words, old wounds, and the ghost of every brother who left the movement when things got hard.

I stared at the Qur'an on the shelf.

You ever reach a point where you ask if truth is worth the cost?

Not just in theory.

But in practice. In relationships. In risk.

"We confront it," I finally said. "Not in their boardrooms. In ours. In public. On record."

Isa's voice lowered. "You sure?"

"I'm done hiding. And I'm done letting him wear our scars like souvenirs."

The line went quiet again before Isa said, "Then let's burn the script."

The night of the event felt like Eid and a trial rolled into one.

Parking was full by Maghrib. We hadn't even unlocked the front doors, and folks were already crowding the sidewalk, some in dashikis, others in hoodies, a few in suits like they were walking into a courtroom ready to testify.

Inside, the air buzzed.

The chairs weren't just filled—they were bracing for something. Sisters took front rows. Uncles sat near exits. Teens hovered in corners with cameras and charged batteries. You could feel it in your chest—this wasn't just a panel.

This was memory.

This was testimony.

This was us, finally naming the pain we'd survived.

Rasheeda opened it up with Qur'an. Her voice didn't shake, even when her eyes did. She recited with the calm of a woman who had already buried too many dreams and was done pretending.

Then Bilal stepped up.

He didn't use notes. Didn't need them.

"I remember the first time we tried to explain our movement to a grant panel," he said. "They asked what made us different. I said: we don't organize around pain. We organize around what pain taught us."

The room stilled.

He went on. About betrayal. About brotherhood. About how a movement is only as strong as the silence it refuses to keep.

Bronx followed.

He didn't talk numbers. Didn't talk programs. He told the story of a kid he mentored who came back from juvie and said, "I don't need another speech—I need to know you're not gonna disappear."

"And we didn't," Bronx said. "Even when we wanted to."

Then came Ameer. Then Isa. Then one of the sisters from Rasheeda's reading circle who spoke like she'd been holding truth in her chest for years, waiting for someone to hand her a mic.

I closed the night.

Not with a speech. Just a confession.

"I was scared," I said. "Scared that if we told the truth, we'd lose everything. But silence didn't protect us. It just prolonged the damage."

I looked at the crowd. Then down at my daughter sitting beside Sara. Then back up.

"This isn't the story of how we were betrayed. This is the story of how we refused to stay broken."

The room didn't clap.

They stood.

Some with fists. Some with tears. Some just whispering du'a.

And in that moment, I knew:

The Professor could keep his lectures.

We had the people.

And no matter what happened next—

we were no longer afraid to speak.

Chapter Twelve

The Things We Carry

The thing about holding it all together is that people eventually forget you're holding anything at all.

They stop asking how you are. They assume the smiles mean strength. They mistake consistency for invincibility.

I had been consistent.

Faithful. Present. Anchored. But inside? Inside I was somewhere between exhausted and invisible.

I couldn't even name when the shift happened. One day I was the brother folks called for advice, the father whose kids ran to the door when he came home, the husband who left sticky notes on coffee mugs just to make her smile. Now? I was a moving part. A trusted routine. A familiar shadow.

Don't get me wrong—Sara loved me. I never doubted that. But love's presence doesn't always cancel loneliness.

We hadn't had a date in months. Not a real one. Not the "Netflix on mute while folding laundry" kind or the "grab takeout and talk about the kids' schedule" kind. I meant the kind where you look each other in the eyes long enough to remember why you chose each other in the first place.

Lately, it felt like we were co-pilots more than partners—both flying the same plane, but never speaking unless something was on fire.

And even then, the conversation came with disclaimers.

Sara had been soaring lately. New circles. New podcasts. Convert mentoring. Sisters' panels. She was blossoming—and I was proud. But I'd be lying if I said that pride didn't come with a little ache.

I missed her.

Not her presence. She was around plenty. I missed the intimacy that came before the movement. Before the kids. Before we were too tired to notice the space growing between us.

One night after a long day of school inspections, emergency board calls, and a parent complaint about "too much Black history in the curriculum," I came home hoping to sit down and say nothing. Just be.

But she was already mid-Zoom call. Headscarf wrapped tight, expression firm, posture polished. She was explaining something about spiritual identity and reclaiming the narrative for new Muslims. Her voice was passionate. Her words sharp.

I stood in the hallway for a while, watching her like a stranger. She was magnetic. Unshaken. Glorious.

And suddenly, I felt like a bystander to my own life.

Later that night, I tried to start a conversation.

"Hey… maybe this weekend we could—"

"I know, babe," she said, not looking up. "We need time. I want that too. Just let me finish this outline and I'll come to bed."

I nodded. But I knew she'd fall asleep at her desk. Again.

I sat on the edge of the bed alone. Just me and my unspoken needs.

I didn't want attention.

I wanted presence.

I didn't want help.

I wanted softness.

And I didn't want her to stop changing the world.

I just wanted to know there was still space for us in the version of it she was building.

Bronx had always been the immovable one.

The brother who stood like a stone wall while chaos danced around him. You needed something lifted, carried, guarded—Bronx was there. No complaints. No drama. Just presence.

But lately, his presence felt… spectral.

He still showed up—meetings, brunches, late-night calls—but he was a fraction of himself. His laugh came half a second late. His shoulders sagged more than usual. His fists clenched more often than they swung.

Rasheeda mentioned he wasn't eating much. Said she made him a full plate one night and he just picked at the rice before sliding the food into a Tupperware "for later." But she found it in the fridge untouched a week later.

That's when I knew it was time to check in.

I told him I'd drop by for a "quick check-in," but I brought a bag of groceries and an extra hoodie just in case I had to stay the night. I knew the signs. When men like Bronx go quiet, it's rarely because there's nothing to say—it's because the words got stuck somewhere behind shame and survival.

His apartment was dim when I walked in. Smelled like too much air freshener and not enough food. A candle burned low on the counter. The place was clean—too clean. The kind of spotless that happens when someone's trying to distract themselves from the mess inside.

"Didn't know you were coming with reinforcements," he said, nodding at the grocery bag.

I raised an eyebrow. "You think I was about to let you starve on my watch?"

He smirked, but it didn't reach his eyes.

We sat on the floor with a few reheated samosas and a bottle of lukewarm ginger beer. No music. No TV. Just the weight of everything neither of us wanted to say first.

Eventually, I broke the silence.

"You feel like talking?"

"Not really," he said. Then he paused. "But I might need to."

I waited.

"I don't know what's wrong with me," he finally said, voice low. "I've been doing all the right things. Showing up. Training the youth. Praying. Reading. But inside? I feel like I'm sinking. Like… I'm the one person nobody expects to fall apart, so I'm trying not to out of loyalty."

That hit hard.

He stared at the candle for a moment, then added, "Sometimes I get in the car and just drive. No music. No destination. Just trying to outrun my own head."

I nodded slowly. "What are you running from?"

He looked at me, eyes glassy.

"The silence."

We didn't speak after that for a while.

Just sat there, chewing slowly, letting the room hold us.

Because sometimes that's all you can do—be near the fire without expecting to put it out.

And for men like us? That's love.

Bilal never liked to talk about feelings.

He'd rather talk legal strategy, protest coordination, or Qur'anic etymology. He could dissect a verse in three languages and expose a city council budget scam before breakfast. But ask him how he's doing—really doing—and he'd respond with a shrug, a smirk, or a subject change.

That's why when I found him sitting on the masjid steps after Fajr, still in his kufi and hoodie, head tilted toward the sky like he was looking for answers in the clouds, I knew something was off.

"You waiting on Jibril from the Qur'an or just hoping I brought coffee?" I joked as I sat down next to him.

He cracked half a smile. "Man, I'm tired of being the thinker."

I didn't push.

"You ever think about disappearing?" he asked, his voice barely above a whisper.

"Every other Wednesday," I said, and we both chuckled.

He leaned forward, elbows on knees. "There's a sister at the mosque. Widow. Two kids. Smart. Witty. She asks questions after halaqa like she's auditing my soul. I think… I think she wants me to propose."

"And?"

"I don't know," he said. "I don't know if I've got anything left to give. My last marriage felt like a war no one declared but everybody lost. I'm scared, Jibril. Scared I'll give her my ruins and she'll mistake it for a blueprint."

That line stopped me.

We were quiet for a long time, both of us staring out at the parking lot as the morning sun threatened to make us visible again.

"I don't know if love is still… available," he added. "Or if it's just something polite people keep trying out of habit."

I reached over and squeezed his shoulder.

"Maybe it's not about finding love," I said, "maybe it's about building something soft enough that it survives the fire next time."

He looked at me like that idea had never occurred to him.

"Or maybe," he said slowly, "we just need to stop confusing love with rescue."

That one landed.

And neither of us had the energy to respond.

So we just sat there, two tired men in the rising sun, hoping forgiveness came with caffeine and that maybe—just maybe—healing didn't always have to be loud.

Khalid was still learning how to be outside.

He'd been with us for a few months—joined quietly, sat at the edges of our gatherings like a man still reading the room. He rarely spoke unless asked. Rarely ate unless offered twice. But when he did speak, you felt it. The man carried weight.

You don't spend two decades inside without learning to sit in silence so deep, it echoes back your own name.

At first, the brothers were cautious. Not because he wasn't welcome, but because trauma wears different cologne. And Khalid's walked in the room before he did.

But slowly, he began to melt into the circle. Shared quotes from scholars. Cleaned up after events without being asked. Showed up on time—always.

He was the kind of man who offered his back before he offered his opinion.

Then one Sunday brunch, he finally spoke.

We were talking about reentry—the slow, awkward crawl back into life after things fall apart. Bronx had just shared something about losing his sense of home after his injury. Bilal mentioned how his divorce had left him allergic to peace and silence. I was halfway into a thought about parenthood when Khalid cleared his throat.

We turned.

He never cleared his throat unless he had something worth saying.

"I been Muslim for 14 years," he began. "Took shahadah inside. Led Jummah for six of those years. Taught brothers who could barely read how to pronounce Surah Fatiha. Memorized juz Amma in the dark with rats scratching behind the radiator."

Nobody blinked.

"But out here?" he said, shaking his head slowly, "out here it's like none of that mattered. I walk into a masjid and get looked at like I brought the prison with me. Like I'm carrying some invisible stain they hope doesn't rub off."

The table went still.

"You know what hurts the most?" he continued. "It's not the stares. I expected that. It's when the people who claim to believe in redemption make you feel like you only belong if you shrink."

Silence.

Then he added, almost as an afterthought: "My son's eleven. Asked me last week why I pray five times a day if I still don't got a job, a car, or a place to call ours."

He paused.

"Wanted to tell him prayer ain't about reward—it's about survival. But I didn't. I just said, 'Because Allah hasn't stopped believing in me. So I won't stop either.'"

The table didn't move.

We didn't have answers.

Just slow nods. And the kind of silence that meant respect, not pity.

Because Khalid wasn't asking for sympathy.

He was offering a reminder.

That faith doesn't always come dressed in victory. Sometimes it comes in hand-me-downs and parole papers. Sometimes it walks in late, sits in the back, and still makes angels weep.

Chapter Thirteen
A House Divided

Some houses don't fall apart all at once.

They shift. They creak. They lean just a little harder in one direction, like they're trying to whisper, "Pay attention before I collapse."

That's what our house felt like that week.

No slammed doors. No shouting matches. Just slow, steady silences—ones that hummed like tension in drywall. Ones that crawled between spaces where laughter used to live.

Sara wasn't angry.

And that's what scared me the most.

Anger I could handle. Raised voices meant she still had the energy to fight, to demand, to insist we come back together. But this? This calm, this distant kindness? It felt like a mercy wrapped around a slow goodbye.

She still did the things that made our house a home—kissed the twins' foreheads with dua, reheated dinner when I was late, reminded me about my mother's birthday. But it was all mechanical now. No softness in the way she folded my hoodie. No pause in her step when I walked in the door. Just… functions. Fulfilled. Efficient. Empty.

And I had no idea how to fix it.

The more I tried, the more misplaced it all felt.

I brought home her favorite chocolate—she didn't touch it.

I offered to take the kids out for the day—she said, "No, they need you too."

I sat beside her one night after the kids went down, hands itching to reach for hers. Instead, I asked, "How was your week?"

She looked up from her laptop just long enough to blink.

"Busy," she said. Then went back to typing.

I wanted to scream. Or cry. Or ask her to put it all down and see me. But instead I nodded, as if "busy" was enough of a conversation for people who'd once whispered dreams into each other's palms.

That night, I slept on the edge of the bed. Not because she told me to. Because I didn't know if I was welcome in the center anymore.

The next morning, Rasheeda stopped by.

She had that look—headscarf pinned sharp, voice sweet, but her eyes were scanning the whole house like a forensic analyst.

"You eat today?" she asked.

I nodded.

She raised an eyebrow. "What'd you eat?"

I paused. "A banana and a leftover juice box."

"Mmhm." She pushed a Tupperware into my hands like it was a prescription. "This is lentil soup. And a proverb."

I laughed, but she didn't.

"A man," she began, "has to know when he's juggling blessings and when he's mismanaging them."

I blinked. "That's... oddly specific."

She stirred the pot on the stove like she hadn't just delivered a diagnosis disguised as dinner.

"I'm trying," I said. "But it feels like no matter what I do, it's never enough. I'm working, organizing, helping with the kids—"

"But are you seeing her?"

"I see her every day."

"No," she interrupted. "Are you seeing the woman behind the scarf, behind the smile, behind the schedule? Or are you just showing up like one more thing on her to-do list?"

That one hurt.

But it was true.

Sara wasn't just tired—she was lonely. And I had mistaken her busyness for fulfillment.

I thanked Rasheeda and sat with her words for hours. They didn't simmer like soup. They burned.

Because somewhere between leadership meetings, late-night school emails, and early morning diaper changes, I had stopped showing up as a husband. I'd become a partner in logistics, not love.

And I wasn't sure when—or if—I could find my way back.

Bronx had always been fire.

Not the destructive kind, but the kind you gather around when everything else is cold.

But lately, his flame had been flickering—unsteady, unpredictable. And we all felt it.

He moved out again. Said it was "temporary." But temporary things have a way of stretching into permanence when pride is louder than pain.

I visited him a few days after he left.

His new place was a studio wedged between a corner laundromat and a vape shop, the kind of building where the hallway lights hum and the elevator buttons are mostly decorative. Inside, it smelled like fresh paint and microwave dinners. Not home. Just… hiding.

"You sure you okay here?" I asked, looking around.

"It's quiet," he said, tossing his keys into a bowl like a man trying to convince himself.

Quiet wasn't always good. Quiet made room for thoughts that didn't knock before entering.

There were no photos on the wall. Just a prayer rug folded neatly on the counter and a Qur'an beside it—like someone had set up a shrine in the middle of a personal storm.

"You heard from her?" I asked.

"Sakeena?" he said, not looking at me. "Yeah. Saw her at the market."

"And?"

"She didn't even say salaam."

The pause after that held more weight than anything either of us said next.

"I don't blame her," he added. "She probably thinks I gave up."

"Did you?"

He sighed. "No. But I stopped fighting for the us that no longer existed. And maybe that feels the same."

We sat in the silence for a while. Bronx rubbed his thumb over a chip in the mug he was holding, like he was hoping it would tell him how to put the pieces back together.

"She said she didn't recognize who I was anymore," he continued. "And the worst part is—I think I agreed."

I wanted to tell him he was still the man who showed up for everyone, still the brother who mentored kids with more trauma than tools. But I knew none of that mattered if the person he loved most thought he'd vanished.

Then he said something that sat on my chest for days.

"You ever get so used to surviving that you forget how to be loved?"

Things with Bilal weren't much better.

Their truce had thinned to a thread—tight, tense, and seconds from snapping.

It started with suspicion. Bilal, already wound tight from failed committees and mounting pressure, had grown watchful. He'd started asking Bronx about old contacts, pushing too hard on details that didn't matter—or didn't seem to. Bronx felt the heat and responded in kind: silence, deflection, absence.

I tried to bridge it.

One afternoon I invited both of them to lunch at the community garden project we'd just launched. Public setting. Peaceful energy. Good food.

It started fine. Small talk. Some laughter. But then Bilal made an offhand comment.

"I just think we should know where our blind spots are," he said, sipping his tea.

Bronx tilted his head. "That your way of saying I'm a risk?"

"I'm saying transparency's a two-way street."

Bronx stood up. "Funny how that street always has cameras when I'm walking on it."

He walked out before the check even came.

Bilal didn't apologize. Just watched him go and muttered, "He's not the same."

Neither were any of us.

And the trust we'd once held like sacred scripture?

It was fraying—one assumption at a time.

Bilal was a man built for war.

Not the bloody kind, but the kind fought in meeting rooms, courtrooms, and community forums. He was at his best when he was pushing against pressure—when he had a target, an injustice to expose, a crowd to rally.

But now? The crowd had grown tired. The injustice more slippery. And the spotlight he once commanded had started to flicker.

And Sahara… she wasn't built for war.

Not anymore.

She had stood beside him for years, carried his vision like it was her own, helped draft statements and plan strategy meetings between diaper changes and postpartum fatigue. But something had shifted.

Maybe it was the baby. Or maybe it was losing people who were supposed to be permanent. Maybe it was just the natural evolution of a woman who was done being a footnote in someone else's mission.

Whatever it was, it showed.

She moved softer these days. Spoke less. Asked Bilal questions he didn't always know how to answer.

"What happens if the movement doesn't win?" she asked him one night, according to Rasheeda. "Do we still have a life?"

He had no response.

Because in his world, there was no plan B.

You either built the better future, or you lived in ruins.

She started spending more time with her mother. Brought the baby with her most weekends. Told Bilal it was just to give him space to focus.

But even space has a sound.

And the silence between them grew louder.

One afternoon, I found Bilal pacing the masjid hallway after Asr. He looked like he hadn't slept—shirt wrinkled, eyes red.

"She's slipping," he said. "I can feel it."

"You talk to her?"

He nodded. "Tried. But everything I say sounds like a pitch now. Like I'm selling her a future she doesn't believe in anymore."

He paused. "She wants stability. But I can't promise that. Not in this line of work. Not when your whole existence is a protest."

He sounded more like a soldier than a husband.

And maybe that was the problem.

That same night, I opened the email again.

The one from the school in Atlanta.

Every word read like a balm: "We believe in your vision." "We want to give you the tools to do this your way." "You won't have to fight to prove your value."

The salary was more than I'd ever seen.

The housing stipend came with a photo of a townhouse wrapped in trees and sunlight.

And the email ended with three words that haunted me: "It's your time."

Sara didn't know I was still considering it.

At least, I thought she didn't.

But the way she moved lately—packing and unpacking suitcases, updating resumes, making quiet lists in her phone—told me she had already built two versions of our life. One here. And one there.

I stared at the screen like it held a moral question.

Because it did.

If I left, I could start over. Heal without the daily reminder of failure. Teach freely. Lead quietly. Raise my children in a city where my name didn't carry past mistakes like echoes in a hallway.

But I'd also be abandoning more than location.

I'd be leaving a movement that still needed mending.

And a brotherhood still struggling to believe in itself.

Escape is always easiest when you've convinced yourself the fight no longer needs you.

But part of me knew…

The fight wasn't over.

Not by a long shot.

Rasheeda had a way of knowing things before you told her.

Not like a spy. More like a mother with divine Wi-Fi. She moved through rooms with both awareness and mercy—listening without eavesdropping, watching without waiting to pounce.

So it didn't surprise me when she said it out loud.

"I know about Atlanta."

She said it while stirring lentils, as if she'd just remembered to mention something minor—like running out of cumin or needing more laundry detergent.

I was standing in the doorway of the kitchen, trying to figure out if this was a trap or an invitation.

"I wasn't snooping," she added. "The email popped up when I was using your tablet to read Qur'an."

I nodded slowly. "I believe you."

She kept stirring. "You thinking about taking it?"

"Every day."

She didn't flinch. Didn't look up. Just stirred a little longer, like she was giving herself permission to respond with something real.

"I get it," she said finally. "You're tired. This place keeps bleeding you, and all they offer in return is more bandages."

That hit.

She turned the stove off and sat at the small table near the window. Gestured for me to sit too.

I did.

"I'd go with you," she said. "If that's what you decide. I'll pack a bag, hug my mother goodbye, kiss this city's broken sidewalks, and follow you to a place with clean air and fewer ghosts."

"But?"

"But don't go if the only reason you're leaving is to run."

She didn't say it like an ultimatum. She said it like a prayer disguised as advice.

"You think I'm running?"

"I think you're hoping peace lives somewhere else. But what if it's not a place?" She looked me dead in the eyes. "What if peace is just unfinished business being mistaken for failure?"

I looked down. "I'm tired of fighting."

"Then fight differently," she said. "Build slow. Breathe. Say no more often. Ask for help. You don't have to bleed to prove you're worth saving."

We sat in that quiet for a while.

She didn't push. Just placed her hand over mine and said, "I want you to choose joy, Jibril. Not just duty. And I want you to remember who you were before you had something to prove."

That one cracked something open in me.

Because I had forgotten.

Forgotten the young me who just wanted to teach kids truth without begging for funding.

Forgotten the man who dreamed of building something honest, even if it was small.

Forgotten the brother who prayed with reckless hope and believed every ayah about Allah seeing effort over outcome.

And Rasheeda saw all that in me.

Still.

Even when I didn't.

Bronx came by unannounced.

No text. No call. Just a knock on the front door like it still belonged to him—and maybe it did.

I opened it, and there he stood—hoodie half-zipped, a paper bag of takeout in one hand, and something heavy sitting in his eyes. He looked like a man who hadn't slept, but didn't want to talk about it.

"Figured you hadn't eaten," he said, holding the bag up like a peace offering.

I stepped aside.

We didn't say much while we unpacked the food. Falafel, fries, some strange but delicious eggplant wrap. The kind of food you bring when you want to fill the space with something—anything—other than the truth.

We ended up on the front steps, just like old times. Legs stretched. Shoulders slouched. The kind of silence that doesn't need to be broken because it's doing exactly what it's supposed to do.

Then he said it.

"She didn't even say salaam."

"Sakeena?"

He nodded. "Ran into her at the market. We were less than six feet apart, and it was like I was air."

I didn't know what to say. So I just said, "That hurts."

He let out a long breath. "Yeah."

He stared straight ahead like he was looking at a memory he hadn't finished unpacking.

"But I don't blame her," he added. "I mean, I wish she could see I'm still trying. That I haven't stopped showing up. But maybe I didn't show up when it counted most. And that's the kind of absence you can't apologize your way out of."

That sat heavy between us.

"I'm hurting too," he continued, "but I'm trying not to let it turn me cold. I keep reminding myself—if I can't be forgiven, I can still be accountable."

I reached out and clapped his shoulder.

"You're still in the fight, brother. That counts."

He nodded slowly. "Sometimes I think the real fight ain't the protests, the school board meetings, or even the movement. It's this—sitting with your shame, your regrets, and choosing not to disappear. That's the war."

He looked over at me and asked what I'd been dreading.

"You leaving?"

I didn't answer right away.

"I might," I finally said.

He didn't flinch. Didn't plead.

"If you do, I get it," he said. "But if you stay… I'll stay too."

That cracked something in me.

He kept going.

"Not because everything's fixed or even fixable. But because somebody's got to be here when the smoke clears. Somebody has to say, 'We didn't abandon it. We didn't abandon each other.'"

I looked out at the street, the shadows growing longer.

"You ever feel like we're just survivors dressed up like leaders?" I asked.

He laughed quietly. "Every day. But maybe that's the beauty of it. We're not pretending we've got all the answers. We're just refusing to let go of the questions."

The porch light flicked on. We didn't move.

And I realized something in that moment—maybe staying isn't about being stuck. Maybe it's about becoming the kind of man who can finally face what he's been running from.

The truth. The pain. The love he thought he lost. The future he's still scared to claim.

Sometimes, staying is the most radical thing you can do.

And Bronx, just by showing up…

reminded me how.

Chapter Fourteen

Smoke Before the Fire

It wasn't the arguments that worried me.

Arguments meant something was still burning. They meant you cared enough to raise your voice, to push back, to risk discomfort for the sake of connection.

No, it was the silence that haunted me.

Bronx and I had been working together nearly every day—project check-ins, community checklists, meetings about youth mentorship, school programming—but it had been days since he'd cracked a joke or asked a real question. His words were minimal. Efficient. Civil. And cold.

Like someone who had learned to smile through frostbite.

I noticed it first during our site walkthrough at the new youth center. Normally, Bronx was the first to suggest something—where to place the punching bags, how to space out the prayer room, where to install security cameras. But this time? Nothing. He walked behind me, nodded a lot, and stared off into corners like they held secrets I couldn't access.

"You like the layout?" I asked.

He shrugged. "It's cool."

That was it.

Cool.

This was a man who once wept when we got a vending machine installed in a school library. Now he could barely muster a response to a project we dreamed about during overnight halaqas and kitchen-table blueprints.

At first, I told myself it was stress. Maybe Sakeena. Maybe exhaustion. But it wasn't just one thing. It was all the things—stacked, unspoken, simmering. And now, the man who used to speak with fire was burning inward, and I didn't know how to reach him.

At one point, I almost pulled him aside after a meeting. Almost.

But then I looked into his eyes—tired, unreadable—and I knew I'd just get a head shake or a tired, "I'm good."

So I let it go.

And that haunted me too.

Because when you've built something with a brother—bled, prayed, rebuilt, forgiven—it changes you. It rewires your soul around their presence. And when that connection dulls, even without drama, it cuts like a blade dipped in ice.

Later that evening, I called Rasheeda.

"Has he said anything to you?" I asked.

There was a pause on the line. Then: "Only when necessary."

"How's he holding up?"

She sighed. "Like someone afraid to grieve. Afraid that if he does, he won't stop. I hear him pacing at night. Not angry. Just… searching."

That word—searching—hit me in the chest.

Because I was searching too.

And lately, I didn't know if either of us could find our way back.

There's a kind of grief that doesn't come from death.

It comes from watching something sacred decay in slow motion.

That's what was happening between Sakeena and Bronx. Not a blowup. Not a betrayal. Just a slow, steady erasure of what once lived between them.

They hadn't had a real conversation in over a week—not one that wasn't about the boys, groceries, or bedtime schedules. They were operating like a joint task force now: coordinated drop-offs, shared calendars, mutual politeness. It was professional. Efficient. Respectful even.

And it was killing them.

Bronx had moved into the guesthouse behind Rasheeda's duplex a month ago, saying he "just needed space to think." Sakeena didn't argue. She just nodded like a woman too tired to resist one more unraveling.

Now they lived like two chapters in a book no one wanted to finish. Same property. Different pages.

When I dropped by one afternoon to check on the kids, I saw it for myself. Sakeena answered the door, her face brightening briefly when she saw me.

"Uncle J," she smiled. "Come in. Boys are in the backyard with Ma."

The house was spotless. Not in the show-off kind of way, but in the way people clean when they need control over something. The air smelled like cinnamon and eucalyptus. It felt staged—like comfort had been set up, but not lived in.

As we sat, she poured me tea. I watched her move with grace and efficiency. Not an ounce of wasted motion. But behind her eyes… fog.

"You doing okay?" I asked gently.

She nodded. "Just tired. Managing. It's a lot."

I didn't press. Not yet.

"How's Bronx holding up?" I ventured.

She looked down at her tea, stirring it long after the sugar had dissolved.

"We don't really talk about feelings anymore," she said quietly. "Just tasks."

She smiled faintly—sad and practiced. "I used to dream in color. Now I schedule in grayscale."

I didn't know what to say to that.

I wanted to say, He still loves you, but that would've been dishonest. Not because the love wasn't real, but because sometimes love gets buried under so much regret that even the people who feel it can't reach it anymore.

Before I left, she walked me to the door and added something that lingered with me the rest of the day.

"I think we're both just trying to be functional. But the cost of function… is feeling nothing at all."

And I couldn't help but wonder…

How many Black Muslim families had become expert co-survivors instead of intimate partners?

How many of us had settled for structures over soul?

And what would it take to revive something that once lived in full color— but now whispered only in beige?

The flyer showed up in our group chat like an unexpected slap.

There was no message. No context. Just the image:

"The Future of Black Muslim Leadership: A Call to Power"

Presented by: The Ummah Vanguard Collective

And there he was—front and center.

Bilal.

Arms folded. Jaw set. Eyes blazing with that unmistakable intensity.

It wasn't the photo that shook me—it was the tagline below it:

"We don't need saviors. We need systems."

Classic Bilal. Smooth. Subversive. Revolutionary and provocative all at once.

He'd been silent for weeks. No texts. No updates. Just gone. And now? A full-fledged initiative with an official name, a flyer, and an event date. It was like watching someone you used to build houses with move across the street and build a mansion without even telling you they were buying land.

I showed Bronx.

He stared for a long time before handing my phone back.

"Guess we'll see what that's about."

That was it. No rage. No sarcasm. Just the voice of a man so used to betrayal that even disappointment had gone numb.

I couldn't help but feel it too—not just the sting of being left behind, but the ache of being replaced. Bilal wasn't just building something new—he was doing it without us. Without the men who bled beside him. Who prayed next to him. Who helped him bury pieces of himself after every loss.

Part of me was proud. He hadn't quit. He hadn't crawled into the shadows. He was rising again.

But the other part—the part that still felt the scar from our last fallout—felt betrayed.

Because we were supposed to rebuild together.

Now we were just pages in each other's archives.

To make it worse, the keynote speaker listed below his name made my blood run cold:

"Featuring Professor Kareem."

No photo. Just the name.

The man we had cut ties with. The man who cost us lives, money, credibility—and almost each other.

And now Bilal had invited him back into the spotlight.

I stared at the flyer for a long time, trying to decide if this was an act of desperation, brilliance, or both.

That night I barely slept.

I kept replaying every late-night conversation I ever had with Bilal.

Every strategy session.

Every whispered dua in hotel lobbies.

And I wondered how a man so loyal, so fireproof, could now be standing next to the very flame we'd all agreed would never be relit.

The brothers were already in their seats when she walked in—long navy trench coat, soft leather messenger bag, and round glasses that gave her a scholar's gravity before she even opened her mouth.

Soraya Malik.

Thirty-something. Kenyan-American. Ph.D. candidate in Islamic Law with credentials long enough to stretch across continents. She'd worked in refugee camps, lectured in international forums, and mentored more young Muslim women than most masjids could claim as members. But none of that was what made the room sit up.

It was her presence.

She walked in like she didn't need permission.

She didn't adjust herself to make anyone comfortable.

She didn't wait for a cue.

"Before we talk funding," she said, setting down her bag and looking directly at us, "I'd like to ask—how many of you are prepared to be students yourselves?"

The room froze.

I heard a pen click. Someone shifted in their chair.

"I'm serious," she continued. "You can't build a movement on emotional appeal and nostalgia. If you want a curriculum rooted in Black Muslim scholarship, start with yourselves. Read. Write. Learn Arabic if you haven't already. Show these boys it's possible. Or are you expecting it all to be outsourced again?"

Ameer let out a low whistle. "Well then."

I suppressed a smirk.

Most of the brothers were caught somewhere between impressed and irritated. Her delivery wasn't aggressive—but it was unapologetic. And we weren't used to that from newcomers, especially not women who didn't spend the first ten minutes softening their edges.

But I loved it.

She wasn't here for approval. She was here to build.

Bronx sat with arms folded, jaw tight. Isa looked intrigued, if a little threatened. Abdul muttered something under his breath about "manners," but didn't speak up.

When the meeting ended, I lingered.

She was repacking her bag, adjusting her scarf, calm as a woman with nothing to prove.

"Can I ask your honest take?" I said. "About what you saw in there."

She paused for a beat, then looked me in the eye.

"You have the bones of something remarkable," she said. "But your house is cracked. Too many unresolved grudges. Too many chiefs trying to prove they were right. Not enough workers willing to admit they're still students."

She didn't need to name names. I knew exactly who she meant. Including myself.

"And Professor Kareem?" I asked.

Her expression changed, but only slightly.

"I've read his papers," she said. "He's brilliant. Dangerous. Charismatic. He speaks revolution, but he builds empires—for himself."

That landed hard.

Because we had lived it. And we were still bleeding from it.

She closed her bag and added, almost as an afterthought, "Don't confuse strategy with sincerity. A man can say all the right things and still be pointing you in the wrong direction."

And just like that, she left.

Didn't wait for applause. Didn't look for affirmation. Just walked out like she had somewhere more important to be than the fragile egos of well-meaning brothers.

And I couldn't help but think…

Maybe she was the first real leader we'd seen in months.

The gym lights flickered as I stepped outside, towel slung over my shoulder, body sore but mind still buzzing from the meeting with Soraya. The air was thick, humid—one of those Houston nights where even the wind felt like it had something to say.

Bronx was sitting in his car. Engine off. Radio silent.

I didn't knock or ask. I just opened the passenger door and slid in beside him.

We sat like that for a long while.

Two men, soaked in sweat and silence.

"You think she's legit?" he asked eventually, eyes fixed on the windshield.

"Soraya?"

He nodded.

I leaned back in my seat. "Seems that way. She's got clarity. Nerves of steel. And she doesn't seem impressed by anyone's titles."

"She got under my skin," he muttered.

I raised an eyebrow. "In a bad way?"

He shook his head. "Not really. Just… made me feel like I've been floating. Like I'm showing up, but not growing. Not learning. Just… existing."

"You've been healing," I said.

"Yeah, but healing's starting to feel like hiding."

That landed.

I let the silence do its work.

He sighed. "I can't tell if I'm waiting to get better… or if I've already quit."

That one punched me in the chest.

Because I knew that feeling. That blur between recovery and surrender.

"Maybe you just need someone to remind you what you're capable of," I offered.

He gave me a look. "Used to be the Professor."

There it was.

The shadow in the room.

"I don't know what I'll do if I see him again," he said. "I really don't."

I wanted to lie. To say, You'll be calm. You'll be smart. You'll be better than him.

But I couldn't promise that. Not with what we'd all lost. Not with how deep that betrayal ran.

Instead, I said, "If he comes back, we handle it together."

He didn't reply. Just stared straight ahead.

But I could feel it.

Something was coming.

Not loud yet. Not bright. But it was there.

A pulse. A hum. A storm waiting for its cue.

And deep down, we both knew—

The Professor wasn't coming for peace.

And this time?

We weren't sure if we were the students… or the battlefield.

Chapter Fifteen

Pressure Builds in Silence

The city felt tighter than usual.

It wasn't the traffic or the heat. It was something deeper—like the city itself was holding its breath.

And I was too.

Ever since the flyer surfaced with Bilal and Kareem's names side by side, something had shifted in our brotherhood. Not on the surface—no one threw chairs or cursed in group chat. No one walked out of brunch. But the conversations got shorter. The laughter didn't last as long. The meetings ended before the last brother finished his tea.

Even the prayer circles felt different. Softer. Slower. Like we were afraid to say the wrong name out loud.

I noticed it in Bronx first. His "salaams" were solid, but his hugs had gotten one-armed and quick. Like a man guarding his ribs. He still showed up— always the first one there, keys in hand, setting up chairs like clockwork. But his presence had thinned. Like he was there in body, but his soul was already somewhere else, scouting for the next betrayal.

The rest of the brothers weren't far behind.

Abdul—normally the first to speak his mind—had gone quiet, nodding through meetings like a deacon at a service he didn't believe in anymore.

Isa—once the life of every logistics session—stopped sending his weekly updates. When asked, he blamed "new projects," but I could tell he was distracted. Fidgety. Like a man rehearsing two versions of the same speech for two very different audiences.

Even Ameer—our light-bringer, our "what if we just made dua and drank smoothies" optimist—started staying home on Sundays.

And I couldn't blame any of them.

Because I was drifting too.

Not away from the mission, but away from the myth that everything was still okay.

The truth was, the walls of our brotherhood were groaning. Not cracking yet—but close.

What used to feel like a family now felt like a fragile ceasefire.

We all remembered the last time Kareem appeared—how he split us down the middle with charisma and cunning. How he used scripture like strategy and trust like currency. And how it took a near-death, a funeral, and a miracle to come back from it.

So when his name resurfaced—not whispered, but printed boldly on a flyer next to Bilal's—every brother who had lived through the fallout felt the old weight return.

But no one said it.

Because saying it made it real.

And real was terrifying.

He came back like nothing happened.

No warning. No phone call. No text to soften the edge.

Just walked into the brunch spot like he'd only missed a week instead of a month and a half.

Bilal.

Trimmed beard. Pressed thobe. Signature leather satchel over his shoulder. Same old fire simmering behind his eyes, but colder now—less like a flame, more like coals waiting for kindling.

He greeted the brothers warmly—fist bumps, shoulder hugs, inside jokes worn thin with time. No one called him out. No one asked, "Where've you been?"

Because when a man like Bilal disappears, you don't chase him. You just wait to see what he brings back when he returns.

That first brunch, he sat next to me like we hadn't exchanged tense texts or raised voices in a masjid hallway. Like he hadn't gone quiet when we needed his counsel most. He poured me tea.

"Still no sugar?" he asked.

I nodded.

He didn't speak after that.

We sat shoulder to shoulder, chewing quietly, as Abdul told a story about his son mistaking wudu for a science experiment. Ameer chuckled. Isa sipped his juice like it was his only line of defense.

And Bilal?

He just watched.

Watched us all.

The brothers let him blend back in like water returning to a cracked well. But I couldn't.

Not yet.

Later, as we walked out toward the lot, I slowed down so we ended up alone.

"You back for good?" I asked.

He shrugged. "Depends what you mean by good."

I stopped walking. "You know what I mean."

He paused, then turned to face me. "I'm here. That has to count for something."

"I didn't say it didn't. But when you leave and don't explain, it leaves room for assumptions. For doubt."

He nodded slowly, eyes scanning the street like it might offer a better reply than he had.

"I needed time," he said. "To think. To build. And to breathe without every decision being a group vote."

That one stung. Because it was true. And it wasn't.

"You joined Kareem," I said flatly.

"I partnered with a platform," he corrected. "I'm not following him—I'm using him."

"And what if he's using you?"

He didn't answer. Just looked at me with that tired conviction—the kind you develop when you're too proud to admit fear.

"I'm still your brother, Jibril."

"I know."

"But?"

I took a long breath.

"But you can't disappear again. Not without consequence. Not without wreckage."

We didn't hug.

We didn't dap.

We just nodded—the kind of nod brothers give when they're still angry, but the love runs too deep to cut clean.

And as he walked away, I wondered:

Were we all just pretending not to bleed?

Or had we just gotten used to walking wounded?

Sara had been quieter lately.

Not the angry kind of quiet. Not even the tired kind.

It was the kind of quiet that made you nervous because it meant something was shifting—slowly, invisibly, and probably without your permission.

She lingered at the dinner table after the twins were down, sipping lukewarm tea she never seemed to finish. Some nights I'd find her in the dark, scrolling through something on her phone with the brightness turned all the way down, the glow barely reflecting off her glasses. Other nights, she sat with the Qur'an open—not reciting, just staring at it. Like she was asking it a question she was too afraid to speak out loud.

I wanted to ask her what was wrong.

But the truth was, I already knew.

She had been reborn into this faith with beauty and fire—eager, sharp, unapologetically curious. But now? Now she was carrying the weight that comes when the honeymoon ends and you realize the ummah you married into still doesn't know what to do with women like you.

She was asked to speak more often now—at conferences, workshops, women's halaqas. Sisters loved her. Organizers praised her. Masjid boards tolerated her.

But behind all the applause, I could see it.

It was draining her.

"Do you feel seen?" I asked one night as we folded laundry on the couch.

She didn't answer right away.

"I feel… observed," she said finally. "Not seen. Not heard. Definitely not protected."

She didn't say it with bitterness. Just honesty.

I stopped folding and looked at her.

"What can I do better?"

Her eyes softened, but her voice didn't.

"You can remember that I'm not just strong. I'm human. And sometimes, I want to be cared for… without having to earn it."

That cut deep.

Not because I disagreed, but because I hadn't realized how much I'd let her strength excuse my absence.

We spent the rest of the night in silence. But it wasn't the tense kind.

It was the kind where love returns in soft breaths, where apologies are whispered through touch, and where marriage becomes less about performance and more about presence.

Still, as I watched her fall asleep on the couch, Qur'an still open beside her, I wondered—

How many women in our community were carrying the movement on their backs while barely being asked how their hearts were doing?

And how many of us thought our presence was enough, when what they really needed…

was partnership?

It started with six brothers.

Mostly young. College-aged. A few just out of high school. They sat cross-legged on the carpet in the masjid basement with cheap notebooks, cracked phone screens, and eyes that looked more awake than I'd seen in years.

Soraya stood at the front—not behind a podium, not with a microphone. Just standing. Confident. Calm. Coat still on. Glasses slipping down her nose. She opened her crate of books like she was unpacking medicine.

"No PowerPoint today," she said. "We're going to build a syllabus from scratch. Together."

The brothers nodded like soldiers. Ready. Willing.

By the third session, there were fifteen.

By the fifth, there were women, too. A makeshift divider was arranged—nothing formal, just an agreed boundary. No one made a fuss. No uncle came down to interrupt. Because truthfully, no one dared.

She was different.

Not in how she spoke, but in how she didn't apologize for being the most prepared person in every room she entered.

She quoted Qur'an, Malcolm, Ibn Khaldun, Toni Morrison. She wove liberation theory with Islamic jurisprudence like someone who had walked through both and returned with receipts.

I watched one session from the hallway.

I didn't mean to. I had come to drop off some flyers, maybe grab a janazah donation form for an elder who had passed. But I stayed. Leaned against the wall like a ghost of the old guard.

She was teaching them about the political theology of Surah Ash-Shu'ara—the Chapter of the Poets. How revelation used rhythm to confront false kings. How every movement had a soundtrack, and how ours had been missing its beat.

They listened like it was Friday khutbah.

I felt a quiet pride swell in my chest.

But also something else.

Displacement.

For so long, we were the ones who carried the weight of change. Who met in garages, who printed flyers with ink-stained fingers, who dodged city officials and sat through masjid board interrogations.

And now?

Now there was a new voice.

And they didn't need our permission.

Later that evening, I caught her in the hallway, organizing her crates into the back of a weathered hatchback.

"You got a minute?" I asked.

She nodded.

"You're doing good work," I said. "They need you."

She smiled faintly. "They need you too. Don't let the silence convince you otherwise."

I exhaled. "Hard not to feel like the old team got left off the new roster."

She leaned against her car. "Movements aren't rosters. They're rivers. Sometimes the water looks different, but it's still part of the flow."

I laughed. "Did you just turn my existential crisis into a metaphor?"

She shrugged. "It's in the job description."

We both stood there in the fading light.

And I realized I didn't resent her rise.

I just wasn't ready for what it meant:

That leadership wasn't a seat you held—it was a baton you passed.

And if we weren't careful, the race would keep running…

with or without us.

It was a Tuesday evening when it happened.

No hashtags. No livestreams. No city council mentions. Just a flyer.

The town hall had arrived.

"The Future of Black Muslim Leadership: A Call to Power"

The location wasn't a masjid, but a converted library space in Eastwood.

That meant something. Neutral territory. Symbolic turf.

I didn't go in.

Instead, I parked across the street in a borrowed sedan, Rasheeda in the passenger seat. She insisted on coming—not as a sister, but as a strategist. "You can't make sense of power plays from the stage," she'd said. "You need the balcony seat."

We watched.

Brothers arrived in waves. Not our usual circle. Not the ones who bled with us when Black Up was born in a broom closet behind a halal meat shop. These were new faces—young organizers, college poets, grant writers. Dressed sharp. Speaking fast. Holding clipboards like shields.

Security was organized. Not military. But methodical. Matching polos. Walkie-talkies. Coordinated movements. Kareem never liked chaos. Even his revolutions were on a schedule.

A new logo hung from the banner outside:

A clenched fist holding a pen.

Not a sword. Not a rifle. Not even a book.

A pen.

It was brilliant. Subtle. Subversive. He was branding resistance as literacy. Revolution as policy.

"He's not preaching anymore," Rasheeda murmured. "He's pivoting."

"Into what?"

She exhaled. "Into legitimacy."

Then we saw her name on the schedule: Soraya Malik — Guest Scholar.

My stomach turned.

Not because I didn't trust her—but because I hadn't known.

She hadn't told me.

Inside, we could see silhouettes taking the stage one by one. A few short applause breaks. Some laughter. Mostly silence.

Kareem still hadn't shown. But we knew he was there.

His fingerprints were on everything.

Later that night, Bronx dropped a single message in the chat:

"He's back. And he brought receipts."

No one replied.

We didn't need to.

We could all feel it:

This wasn't just a reentry.

This was a recalibration.

He wasn't screaming from the rooftops anymore.

He was whispering from boardrooms.

And the scary part?

People were listening.

The emails started quietly.

No subject lines. No greetings. Just attachments.

First it was a PDF—four pages long, outlining a list of local partnerships with something called the Community Stability Integration Taskforce. At first glance, it looked harmless—some community liaisons, some workshops, a few corporate donors.

But then came the second email.

A spreadsheet.

It included funding streams. Acronyms we didn't recognize. And under the "special allocations" column were titles that sent chills down my spine: Cultural Monitors. Digital Sentiment Analysts. Strategic Influence Facilitators.

It wasn't an organization.

It was a system.

And Kareem had built it under our noses.

He wasn't building masjids or schools. He was building infrastructure— digitally native, grant-backed, data-fed—and aligned with every buzzword that earned favor in city planning meetings.

"Community resilience."

"Interfaith cohesion."

"Preemptive engagement."

All the language of care. All the methods of control.

And the kicker?

He wasn't hiding it.

The documents were polished. Public. Distributed quietly through professional networks, passed around at brunches hosted by nonprofits we used to work with. And the saddest part?

Some of the brothers we trained were already onboard.

Juniors we mentored were listed as "project leads."

One brother—barely 25—was now "Director of Strategic Engagement."

It wasn't betrayal.

It was evolution.

Kareem hadn't come to silence us.

He'd simply moved the game forward.

And left us behind.

I stared at the documents until my eyes blurred. Then I forwarded them to Bronx and Bilal with two words:

"He's winning."

No one replied.

The next morning, I stood in front of our school building with a cup of coffee and a deep ache in my chest.

Not fear.

Not even anger.

Just… recognition.

We had been out-organized.

While we were patching wounds and nursing trust, Kareem had been building systems. While we were mentoring at cookouts and dreaming in whiteboards, he'd been embedding himself in policy circles.

And the community?

It didn't want speeches anymore.

It wanted results.

Even if they came with surveillance.

Even if they came from him.

I sat on the edge of our bed, laptop still open, documents still on the screen. Sara walked in carrying a basket of laundry, humming softly to herself—something she did when she was either deeply at peace or deeply disturbed. I couldn't tell which.

"You're up late," she said.

"Kareem's reinventing the wheel," I muttered.

She set the basket down and sat next to me, glancing at the spreadsheet. It took her less than thirty seconds to understand what she was looking at. Sara was quick like that. Pattern recognition was her superpower. She didn't ask for context.

She just whispered, "He's not building trust. He's buying silence."

I blinked. "What do you mean?"

"He's offering institutions what they've always wanted: a tamed Muslim. Someone polished. Someone articulate. Someone who looks like the resistance but acts like the compliance."

I rubbed my temples. "We're still in the trenches trying to build people, and he's… commodifying them."

Sara leaned forward and scrolled down to one of the documents. "Look at this line item. 'Family engagement workshops focused on behavioral alignment and loyalty frameworks.' That's not education. That's soft control."

I stared at the screen.

Then she said something that stopped me cold.

"This kind of leadership is most dangerous for women."

My eyes met hers. She continued, steady, measured.

"Movements like his tokenize us. They call us 'essential,' 'resilient,' 'backbone of the ummah'—but only when we're convenient. When we raise real questions? When we demand protection and autonomy? Suddenly, we're distractions. Or worse—threats."

I swallowed hard. "You think he's targeting women?"

"No," she said. "I think he's exploiting what most movements ignore. That women, especially Black Muslim women, are the soul of the house and the easiest to erase if the house gets sold to someone else."

I didn't respond right away. I couldn't.

Because she was right.

Everything about Kareem's new model screamed respectability. Polished press releases. Diverse photo ops. Gender equity buzzwords without a single woman in true authority.

Sara continued, her voice quieter now.

"We can't build another movement that needs women's labor but doesn't respect their agency. I'm telling you now, Jibril—if this becomes another boys' club in revolution's clothing, it'll fall apart just like the last one."

I nodded slowly.

Not because I was convinced she was right.

But because I finally realized—

She always had been.

And if we didn't move different?

Kareem wouldn't need to tear us down.

We'd crumble from within.

The call came mid-morning.

Bronx.

"Meet me outside Masjid An-Nur. Now."

No salaam. No explanation.

Just urgency.

I threw on my jacket and drove the fifteen minutes without music, without dua, without distraction—just silence and suspicion.

When I pulled up, he was leaning against a black Honda Civic. Hood up. Head down. Hands in the pocket of a hoodie I hadn't seen him wear since before the fallout with Sakeena.

He didn't say a word until we were both seated inside my car with the windows up.

Then he handed me a phone.

"I took it from a kid who's been hanging around my gym the last few weeks. Said he was volunteering. Asked a lot of questions. Too many. Something felt off."

I unlocked the phone.

The gallery app opened automatically.

Photos.

Of us.

Me at the school. Bronx walking into the masjid. Sara outside the grocery store with the twins. Rasheeda unlocking her car. Even Soraya, caught mid-sentence during a sidewalk conversation.

Each shot was timestamped. Labeled. Cataloged.

It wasn't amateur surveillance.

It was methodical. Professional.

I scrolled in disbelief, stomach tightening with every swipe.

Bronx stared ahead, his fists clenched on his thighs.

"I confronted the kid," he said. "Asked who sent him. He panicked. Said he was working off a stipend—'community engagement monitoring'— told me the program was linked to some kind of research institute."

I already knew.

Kareem.

"He's not just tracking events," I whispered. "He's tracking us."

Bronx nodded. "And not just public stuff. Our kids. Our wives. Our homes."

I shut the phone off and tossed it onto the dashboard.

"This isn't organizing," I said. "It's infiltration."

We sat in silence, the engine off, the air growing thick.

Then Bronx muttered something I hadn't heard from him in a long time.

"I want to burn it all down."

Not metaphorically.

Not passionately.

Just honestly.

I put a hand on his shoulder. Not to calm him, but to anchor myself.

Because deep down?

I wanted to, too.

We met in the back of the old school building.

No group text. No flyer. No agenda.

Just five brothers.

Bronx. Abdul. Isa. Ameer. And me.

The room hadn't been used in weeks. Dust clung to the window edges. A single lamp buzzed in the corner like it was fighting for its last breath. The whiteboard still showed ghost lines of old plans—outlines of dreams we hadn't had time to finish.

We didn't sit in a circle this time.

We sat across from each other.

Divided—not by anger, but by fear. By loyalty. By questions no one wanted to ask.

"I found surveillance photos on a phone taken at my gym," Bronx began, voice low. "Photos of us. Our wives. Our kids. Tagged. Dated."

Isa leaned forward, tension rising. "Taken by who?"

"Some volunteer kid. Said he was getting a stipend. Called it community engagement. Said it was for Kareem's new initiative."

Ameer muttered a curse. Abdul shook his head like someone trying to wake up from a nightmare.

I stood.

"We've been playing defense for months. Hoping Kareem would burn out. Hoping Bilal would come back. Hoping Soraya's involvement wouldn't pull others in."

No one interrupted.

"We kept praying and planning while he was organizing. While we patched wounds, he opened new doors. Not through the streets. Through systems. Grants. Boards. Infrastructure."

Isa's voice was low, unsure. "And people are following. Not because they're brainwashed. But because they're tired. Tired of waiting. He's giving them plans."

I met his gaze. "You think that makes it right?"

"I think it makes it real."

Abdul looked up. "So was Goliath."

The silence that followed was thick enough to bite into.

Then I said it. The thing none of us wanted to say.

"Our revolution has been compromised."

It dropped like a verdict.

Not shouted. Not emotional.

Just… real.

Bronx leaned back, eyes dark. "So what now?"

I looked at them. My brothers. My mistakes. My mirror.

"We build again. Quietly. Carefully. But differently. Not to win. To last."

"No more waiting," Abdul said. "No more nostalgia."

"No more playing respectability politics," Ameer added. "We speak. Loud and clear."

Isa didn't say anything.

But he didn't get up and leave either.

That was enough.

For now.

We closed in dua, each of us whispering our part.

But as I opened my eyes and looked around, I wasn't praying for victory anymore.

I was praying for clarity.

And the courage to follow it—even if it cost us everything.

Chapter Sixteen

Loose Ends, Tight Circles

"I don't trust him," Bronx said flatly, mid-rep, the dumbbells clinking like punctuation.

We were back in our usual rhythm—late afternoon training at the community gym. The weight bench was our therapy couch, the punching bag our confession booth. But today wasn't about muscle memory.

Bronx wasn't just lifting. He was boiling.

"He disappears for two weeks," he grunted, racking the weights with a metallic clank, "comes back with new donors, slick slogans, and suddenly he's the future?"

I tossed a light jab at the suspended bag. Not enough to shake it. Just enough to keep my hands busy.

"He's not stupid," I said. "He knows how to rebrand. He's been grooming the narrative since he got run out the last time."

"Yeah," Bronx muttered, wiping his forehead with a towel, "but this time, he's got new blood behind him. Young cats. Professional cats. And let's not act like Soraya ain't one of them."

"She's not one of them," I said. "She's just… seeing what they're offering."

Bronx looked at me hard. "And what if what they're offering looks better than what we're building?"

That hit different.

We both knew the truth: image was power. Kareem had mastered it. He wasn't shouting from rooftops anymore—he was sitting in roundtables, submitting grant proposals, getting invited to policy summits.

And us?

We were still folding chairs after Friday prayer.

Bronx grabbed his water bottle, leaned against the wall, and dropped his voice.

"There's something else."

I glanced up. I knew that tone. Bronx didn't traffic in speculation unless the smoke was real.

"Isa's been ghosting."

The smoothie bar was nearly empty—just a couple of nurses from the clinic across the street and a delivery driver scrolling through his phone. Bronx and I took the table near the back, out of view but close enough to the exit in case we needed to walk off steam.

"Three weeks," Bronx said, lowering his voice. "That's how long it's been since Isa last answered a call. Skipped two of Soraya's sessions. Missed Friday at the masjid. I texted him a link to the school supply drive flyer and all he sent back was a thumbs-up."

I raised an eyebrow. "Just the emoji?"

"No words. Just that stupid little yellow hand."

I shook my head. "What's your gut telling you?"

"That he's either been compromised or recruited."

I let the silence stretch between us as I sipped a mango-ginger blend. It was bitter at the end, like the conversation.

Isa had always been… diplomatic. Smart. Smooth. Too smooth, maybe. He knew the language of loyalty. He dropped Qur'an like punctuation, translated hadith on the fly, and could explain zoning policy with the same confidence he used to lead prayer. He was valuable—until he wasn't around.

I scrolled through my messages. Last one from him was a quote from Ibn Taymiyyah, followed by "Let me know how I can help."

That was a month ago.

"You think Kareem flipped him?" I asked.

Bronx shrugged. "Kareem don't flip people. He flatters them. Gives them a room with a title and a window view. Tells them they're the new vanguard."

"And what do we offer?" I asked, more to myself than to him.

Bronx smirked. "Headaches, side-eyes, and long meetings with no snacks."

We both laughed.

But only briefly.

Because beneath the joke was a very real fear: that Isa had walked out of the door we built—and into one with more polish and less purpose.

My phone buzzed. Missed call—Sara.

I texted her back: Still with Bronx. All good.

He looked at me sideways. "She still think I'm a bad influence?"

"She never said that."

"She didn't have to."

We both laughed again.

This time, it stuck a little longer.

But not long enough.

Rasheeda's living room had never felt so small.

The couch was full. The floor was covered in prayer rugs, throw pillows, and tension. Ameer leaned against the bookshelf. Bilal sat with his hands clasped, like he was holding onto a prayer he hadn't dared to say out loud. Soraya was seated cross-legged on the carpet, posture straight, eyes scanning. Sakeena stood in the doorway like she was still deciding whether she should've come at all.

Even Bronx looked cornered, pacing near the window like he was waiting on a reason to throw a punch through it.

Rasheeda brought in a tray of dates and hibiscus tea, but didn't stay.

She just set it down, gave me one long look—the kind that said *"Don't let this spiral"*—and disappeared into the kitchen.

I stood.

"Before we talk about anything else," I said, "I need to ask a question. Direct. Simple."

The room stilled.

"Does anyone here know what Isa's really been up to?"

The silence that followed was not accidental. It was loaded.

Then Soraya broke it, slow and sharp.

"He's been advising the professor."

All motion in the room paused.

"Are you sure?" Bilal asked, voice low.

She nodded. "Last week. Closed Zoom call. No video, just initials and voices. But his voice was unmistakable. He was using our talking points—

language we developed in our think sessions. Strategic faith narratives. Grassroots authenticity. Community-first framing. He even referenced a metaphor I used two weeks ago in our halaqa."

Bronx sat down hard. "So he flipped."

"Or maybe he never chose a side," I said.

Ameer crossed his arms. "Told y'all not to trust him. Man came in quoting Qur'an like it was a résumé."

"Let's not throw fire without fuel," I said. "We don't have concrete proof."

"You saying her word ain't concrete?" Bronx snapped.

"I'm saying public accusations without evidence can split the little we have left," I replied calmly. "If we're going to expose anything, it has to be airtight. Irrefutable. Otherwise, it turns into noise."

Soraya nodded. "He's not stupid. If we call him out now, he'll flip it. Make it about ego. About gatekeeping. He'll become the victim."

Sakeena, quiet until now, finally spoke.

"So what do we do in the meantime?"

The room turned to me.

I exhaled slowly.

"We do what we've always done. We serve. Quietly. Consistently. We rebuild the long way. No posts. No public speeches. Just presence."

The room nodded. Even Bronx.

But I could feel it.

We weren't united.

We were aligned.

And those aren't the same.

Not anymore.

We didn't post a single flyer.

No hashtags. No RSVPs. No special guest imams or catered plates.

We just showed up.

Soup kitchens. Book giveaways. Back-to-school drives. Quiet work in loud neighborhoods.

Bronx ran a free self-defense workshop for teenage boys on the east side, his voice booming over a patchy mic in a community rec center where the A/C barely worked. He taught more than how to block punches—he taught how to recognize when you're angry at the wrong person.

Bilal organized a job readiness seminar at the masjid basement. Wore a suit. Brought printed resumes and folders. No one recognized the old version of him—the one who would've thrown a chair before printing a handout. But there he was, showing brothers how to tie ties and shake hands without looking away.

Soraya held a Saturday study circle at the park. Open-air. Co-ed. She translated West African tafsir texts on-site, scribbling Arabic on a whiteboard tied to a jungle gym. Even the uncles didn't interrupt her. They just watched from the sidelines and nodded like something was finally making sense.

And me?

I kept my head down and moved between sites—organizing, troubleshooting, making sure no one burned out. It wasn't flashy. It wasn't strategic. But it was real.

Still, even in the shadows, we weren't alone.

At every event, there was a face we didn't recognize. A phone angled just slightly toward us. A volunteer who didn't speak much. A brother who showed up early and asked too many logistical questions.

Kareem's eyes.

He wasn't trying to shut us down.

He was trying to absorb us.

Co-opt the narrative.

Claim our work in his press releases.

I caught one of the volunteers snapping a photo of Bronx in mid-demo. I asked for his name—he said "Malik" and handed me a card from something called The Urban Alliance for Muslim Advancement. A shell org. Glossy logo. Vague mission.

I pocketed the card and told him we'd reach out.

I wouldn't.

Because I knew what it was.

They weren't building a movement.

They were building a brand.

And we weren't merchandise.

It was nearly midnight when Sara called.

I was sitting in my car outside the school building, engine off, headlights dimmed. Just breathing. Thinking. Praying. Watching the empty lot like it might offer me answers.

The phone buzzed once.

I answered before the second ring.

"You okay?" she asked, her voice softer than usual.

"Yeah," I lied. "Just wrapping up strategy notes."

She hesitated, and I already knew something was coming.

"There's a reporter. From Muslim Insight. She called the house."

I straightened in my seat.

"She say what she wanted?"

"She's doing a piece. Said it's called 'The New Wave of Muslim Leaders.' She name-dropped you. Bilal. Soraya. Bronx."

I didn't speak.

"She wants to profile the shift," Sara continued. "The next generation. Wants to know what separates your circle from Kareem's."

I rubbed my eyes. "What did you tell her?"

"I told her you'd call back. She left a number."

Silence hung between us like a question waiting to land.

I looked out the windshield at the building we fought to keep open. The mural on the wall was half-faded now—Black fists and Qur'anic verses chipped by weather and time.

"We're not ready for that kind of spotlight," I finally said.

"No," she agreed. "But maybe we need it."

I didn't answer.

Not because I disagreed, but because the truth scared me.

We had spent the last year trying to rebuild quietly. Trying to fix what the professor had broken without making a scene. Trying to heal the brothers without making them martyrs. Trying to protect the community without painting a target on our backs.

But now?

Now they were looking at us.

And silence might be mistaken for absence.

Sara's voice softened again. "If they're going to write about Black Muslims, about leadership, about community—don't let them do it without your voice in it."

I parked outside the house.

The porch light was on. The toys were still in the yard. The world hadn't changed.

But I had.

I stepped inside, kissed her forehead, and stood in the hallway for a long time, just watching the girls sleep.

Tomorrow we'd have to speak.

And this time, we couldn't whisper.

We met in the upstairs office of the masjid. The one nobody liked—half-furnished, stuffy, paint peeling in the corner. The AC clicked like a metronome, and someone had forgotten to empty the trash from last Friday's youth night.

But it was quiet. Private.

Bronx leaned against the window with his arms crossed, jaw flexing. Bilal sat in the plastic desk chair, spinning a pen between his fingers like he was deciding whether it should be a weapon.

I stood.

"They're doing a feature," I said. "Muslim Insight. National piece."

Bronx grunted. "And?"

"They want to talk to us."

"About what?" Bilal asked.

"Leadership. Movement. Faith. Influence. Us."

A silence fell. Not resistance—calculation.

"I don't trust press," Bronx said. "You give 'em five minutes of truth and they'll edit it down to a soundbite you spend two years explaining."

"True," I said. "But if we don't say anything, they'll fill the gaps themselves. With rumors. With spin. With Kareem."

Bilal tapped the pen against his leg. "They want conflict. They want drama. Headlines that sell. What they don't want is nuance."

"So what do we give them?" Bronx asked.

I looked at both of them.

"Clarity."

Bronx raised an eyebrow.

"We don't tell the whole story. Not yet. But we speak the truth that matters—about community. About service. About what real leadership costs."

Bilal exhaled. "What if they ask about Isa?"

"Then we do what leaders do," I said. "We protect the house—even from itself. We don't lie. But we don't bleed on the page, either."

"Strategic silence," Bilal said.

"No," I corrected. "Strategic precision."

Bronx looked at me, eyes hard. "And when it's time to tell it all?"

I didn't flinch.

"Then we tell it all. On our terms."

Her name was Amira Nasir.

Young. Sharp. Known in Muslim journalism circles for her interviews that felt like therapy sessions disguised as articles. She had done pieces on incarcerated converts, Black Muslim doulas, and interfaith coalitions that actually worked.

She wasn't tabloid.

But she wasn't soft either.

I called her just after dhuhr, pacing the empty hallway in the school wing, windows cracked to let the heat drift through like a warning.

"Jibril Salaam," I said as she picked up. "You asked for a call."

"Brother Salaam," she said smoothly. "Thank you for making time. I know things have been…active."

She didn't say chaotic. She didn't need to.

"I don't do interviews," I said.

"But you do community," she replied. "And that's what this is. I'm not writing gossip. I'm documenting the split—and the build."

I paused.

"Then let's start with that. There is no split. There's only people choosing different tools to reach the same goal."

She didn't buy it.

"That's noble. But some of those tools are tracking people's families. Others are rewriting the legacy of movements that birthed them."

I didn't respond right away. Instead, I let her statement breathe. Sometimes, silence is the only way to let truth settle.

She continued, softer now.

"I've spoken to young organizers who credit both you and Professor Kareem. They say one gave them language. The other gave them systems. They're asking which one builds the future."

"That depends," I said. "Do you want to be free, or do you just want to be funded?"

That paused her.

"I want people to know what you stand for," she said finally. "Not just what you're reacting to."

"Then quote me on this," I said, stepping toward the window. "We're not building a platform. We're building a people. We don't need everyone to know our names. We just need them to feel our presence when they're hungry, hurting, or healing."

She was quiet. Then—

"That's the kind of quote that makes a headline."

"I'm not here for headlines."

"Then you're exactly who I should be talking to."

We ended the call ten minutes later.

No bombshells. No confessions.

Just clarity.

And that? That was dangerous enough.

Bronx called me after maghrib.

"I found him," he said. "Corner of 19th and Haskell. Masjid Taqwa parking lot. Alone."

"You talk to him?"

"I'm about to."

I grabbed my keys.

By the time I pulled up, the parking lot lights buzzed overhead like they were struggling to stay neutral. Bronx was posted against a light pole, arms crossed. Isa stood across from him, backpack slung, hands open, like a man who came prepared for defense but not for war.

He saw me step out of the car and nodded once. Not sheepish. Not smug. Just… measured.

"I figured you'd come too," he said.

"You been hard to reach," I replied.

"I know."

Bronx's voice cut in—sharper than mine. "Let's skip the warm-up. You with us or with him?"

Isa looked at both of us like a man choosing between two burning buildings.

"I haven't flipped."

"You advising him," Bronx snapped.

"I'm advising a framework," Isa corrected. "One I helped you develop. He's using it now—but I didn't sell it to him. He adapted it."

"You didn't stop him either," I said.

Isa dropped his eyes, then looked up again—this time, not as the smooth brother who quoted policy and Qur'an in the same breath. This time, he looked tired. Like a man trying to keep both hands on a rope that was unraveling.

"You think this is easy for me?" he asked. "I've been in rooms with power I've never seen before—funders, city reps, planners who never looked twice at Black Muslims before Kareem repackaged us into something…manageable."

"That's the problem," I said. "We're not supposed to be manageable."

"You think I don't know that?" Isa stepped forward. "But some of those kids we're mentoring? They're hungry. Homeless. One offer from Kareem's camp and they've got a paid internship and a monthly stipend. Meanwhile, we're scraping together flyers and prayers."

Bronx glared. "So you sold your soul for a direct deposit?"

"No," Isa said quietly. "I sold my comfort for access. And I've been trying to figure out how to undo it without taking everything down with me."

I looked at him.

That was the first time he sounded… real.

"You're still feeding him information?" I asked.

He shook his head. "Not anymore. Haven't been for weeks. He got what he needed. Now he doesn't call. Not unless he wants a quote."

"Then why'd you go silent?" Bronx asked.

Isa looked at the ground. "Because I was ashamed."

We stood in silence for a long moment.

"I can't undo what I gave him," Isa said. "But if you'll let me—I can help stop what comes next."

I looked at Bronx.

He didn't nod.

But he didn't walk away.

And for now?

That was enough.

It was late when I got home.

Too late for excuses, too early for sleep.

The house was still. The twins were down. Imani's backpack was half-zipped by the couch, her sneakers kicked off in the hallway like she'd just outrun the day. The glow from the kitchen light bled gently into the living room, wrapping everything in a kind of peace I hadn't earned yet.

Sara was seated at the table.

Not waiting up for me. Just… there.

Reading. Notebook open. Hijab loosely wrapped like she'd long ago stopped expecting visitors but hadn't given up on modesty.

I slid into the seat across from her and placed my phone facedown.

She didn't look up right away. Just kept writing something—verses or thoughts or maybe a checklist of all the things she carried silently while I was out saving the world.

"You're late," she finally said, not accusing—just observing.

I nodded. "Ran into Isa."

She closed her notebook.

"And?"

"He's not the enemy," I said. "But he's no longer just a friend."

We sat with that.

"Do you ever think," she said slowly, "that this whole thing—Black Up, the Breakfast Club, the organizing, the school—was really just a long way of trying to become the men we wished raised us?"

That hit somewhere I didn't expect.

And couldn't deflect.

"Every day," I said.

She leaned forward, voice soft but surgical. "Then be that man. Not the one who builds systems. The one who shows up. For your brothers. For your kids. For your own heart."

I looked at her—really looked.

And for a moment, I didn't see a wife or a partner or even a pillar.

I saw a mirror.

And I didn't flinch.

I stood outside my daughters' bedroom for a while.

Listened to them breathe.

Counted the seconds between their sighs and the creak of the fan.

This world would not wait for them to grow.

And so I had to become the kind of man who didn't just fight battles—

But built sanctuaries.

With my faith.

With my words.

With my choices.

Because the war wasn't coming.

It was here.

And I wasn't in the shadows anymore.

I was walking in with my eyes open.

And this time, the door between me and the future?

I was ready to walk through it.

Chapter Seventeen

Trust No One

There's a numbness that comes after betrayal—like your blood forgets how to move.

I felt it the second I opened the email.

Subject line: For Your Eyes Only

Sender: a string of random numbers and characters.

Signature: -K.

Kareem. Of course.

I should've deleted it. I should've treated it like the digital poison it was. But men like Kareem didn't send emails unless they wanted you to see something. And I couldn't afford to stay blind.

So I clicked.

Screenshots.

Multiple. Stacked like daggers.

A series of bank transfers—clean but calculated.

Meeting notes—dates, times, names.

A transcript—Isa's voice, unmistakable, advising tone.

"Frame it like community strategy," he said. "That way, it doesn't sound like opposition—it sounds like evolution."

My heart sank.

He had fed Kareem everything: our rebranding efforts, Soraya's media pitch deck, volunteer tracking models, even private reflections I'd shared in a closed brothers' circle.

He hadn't just leaked intel.

He'd betrayed intimacy.

I didn't scream. I didn't text the group. I didn't break anything.

I just closed the laptop.

And drove.

Because sometimes the only way to stop yourself from breaking apart is to put the keys in the ignition and go find the one brother who knows how to sit with your silence.

Bronx opened the door shirtless, sweat still glistening on his shoulders. The scent of metal and chalk dust still clung to his skin. Whatever demons he'd been lifting off his chest hadn't left yet.

"You good?" he asked, reading my face the way only a brother could.

"No," I said, stepping inside. "But I'm coming in anyway."

He didn't say another word. Just nodded once and locked the door behind me.

The apartment was small—just a single couch, some books stacked like barriers around the walls, and a mini-fridge humming in the corner. He tossed me a towel like it was body armor, then sat across from me on the edge of his weight bench.

I handed him the phone.

He scrolled slow. Careful. Like the screen might bite.

When he hit the voice transcript, he leaned back and let out a low, bitter breath.

"Man…"

"I trusted him," I said.

"We all did."

His thumb hovered over the screen. He stared at the last message—Isa advising Kareem on how to subtly absorb our framework without triggering resistance.

"You think Bilal knows?" he asked.

"If he does, he's playing the long game. But I don't think so."

Bronx rubbed his beard, thoughtful. "You trying to bury this or air it out?"

"We can't be quiet anymore."

"Then we burn it down?"

"No," I said. "We light the room."

That got a small smirk from him.

"I like that," he said. "But you better be ready for what crawls out."

"I'm ready."

He stood and grabbed a pen from the counter.

"Then let's write it down. All of it."

We called the town hall on a two-day notice.

No press. No stream. No drama.

Just a quiet summons through trusted threads and word-of-mouth.

By the time we arrived at the rec center, the chairs were full. Ameer was posted by the door, checking names. Rasheeda handled childcare in the back room so the parents could focus. Soraya had a folder on her lap and her eyes fixed straight ahead, her expression unreadable.

Bronx stood to my right. Bilal was two seats over—watchful, arms crossed. Sakeena came and sat in the back. No visible emotion, but she stayed. That meant something.

I didn't use a mic.

I didn't need one.

"I want to speak clearly tonight," I said. "Because the times we're in don't leave room for vague leadership."

The room leaned forward. A few phones were recording silently. I let them.

"There's been a breach. Not of data—but of dignity. Someone we trusted has been passing information to an external entity—an individual known to manipulate movements, divide communities, and build platforms on the bones of those who believed in them."

Gasps. Some heads turned. Others lowered.

I didn't name Isa. But I didn't have to.

I kept going.

"I've seen the receipts. And no, I will not release them. Not yet. Not because I lack courage—but because I believe in mercy. And because I believe our communities deserve solutions, not spectacles."

A pause.

"This ain't about revenge. It's about protection. Of mission. Of community. Of soul."

Someone in the crowd—older, possibly a retired imam—stood.

"What's your plan, Brother Jibril?"

I looked around.

"My plan is not to build empires or crush enemies. My plan is to remind us who we are. Why we started. And who we serve. This betrayal didn't start with us—and if we stay grounded, it won't end with us either."

Bronx stepped forward, just enough to let folks know this wasn't just my stance.

"We're rebuilding," he said. "Not in secret. Not in shame. In service."

A hum of affirmation rolled through the room.

No one applauded.

But no one walked out either.

Which, in our world?

Meant everything.

I found Soraya in the hallway after the town hall, leaning against a faded poster for a long-forgotten food drive. Her arms were folded. Her head lowered just slightly—like someone mourning something still breathing.

"You didn't say his name," she said, not looking up.

"I didn't have to."

"You should have."

Her tone wasn't angry. It was worse—disappointed.

I stepped closer, careful. The hallway lights flickered above us, humming faintly like the past whispering between our words.

"I wasn't protecting him," I said. "I was protecting the movement. The people who still don't know who to trust."

She nodded slowly. "And what happens when silence teaches them to trust no one at all?"

I exhaled.

"I didn't want it to become a witch hunt. Or a circus."

Soraya looked up at me, finally, her eyes sharp but wet around the edges.

"You're not leading a parade, Jibril. You're stewarding a revolution. That means naming poison before it spreads—not after it's already in the bloodstream."

The words hit.

Because she wasn't wrong.

And because I had been dragging my feet trying to protect a fragile balance that no longer existed.

"I just didn't want to give Kareem another headline," I said.

She sighed, softer now. "He already has the headline. He's just waiting to see if you'll write it for him."

We stood there in silence for a beat.

Then she pulled a flash drive from her pocket.

"Everything Isa sent him—dates, files, voice memos—it's all here. My cousin in New York traced the metadata. He masked his IP, but not his signature. Not completely."

I took the drive slowly.

"I want to believe in us," she said. "But belief without accountability? That's just loyalty to pain."

Then she walked past me and disappeared into the night.

And I stood there—

Flash drive in hand.

Heart cracked but awake.

Because maybe this betrayal wasn't meant to break us.

The house was quiet when I returned.

The kind of quiet that presses against your chest—not heavy, just aware. I slipped out of my shoes and found Sara in the kitchen, wiping down the counters. The babies were down. Imani's homework was spread across the dining table like a map of better days.

She didn't ask what happened at the meeting.

She just looked at me. Waiting.

I held up the flash drive.

Her brow furrowed, but she didn't flinch. "From him?"

I nodded. "Soraya tracked everything Isa shared with Kareem. Confirmed it."

Sara didn't say "I told you so." She didn't have to. Her silence wasn't smug—it was solemn.

"Are you going to show the community?" she asked.

I sat at the table, flash drive between my fingers like it weighed more than it should.

"I don't know."

She pulled out the chair across from me and sat slowly.

"What would your father have done?" she asked.

That question landed.

My father. The man who raised me in worn khakis and work boots. Who served quietly. Corrected firmly. Prayed with consistency. He wasn't loud, but he never flinched from truth. When he saw rot in the foundation, he didn't paint over it—he tore it up and laid new brick.

"He would've called it out," I said. "Then done the work to replace what was lost."

Sara nodded. "Then be that man. Not the polished one. The faithful one."

I stared at the flash drive, still turning it slowly.

"There's something else," I said. "A producer from The Ummah Report called me. Wants to do a feature. National audience. Narrative control. It could change everything."

"And Isa?" she asked.

"That's the part I haven't figured out yet."

She reached across the table and touched my hand.

"Then figure it out. Soon. Because the world's watching—even if you're still deciding whether to speak."

Her hand lingered there.

Steady.

Like always.

We met in Bilal's office at the old storefront.

The walls were still bare. One window cracked. A single desk lamp lit the room like an interrogation cell. Bronx stood by the door. Bilal sat at the desk, his laptop closed, hands clasped like he was waiting on a verdict.

I dropped the flash drive on the desk.

"This is it," I said. "Everything he leaked."

Bilal didn't reach for it. He just looked at it—like it might start hissing.

Bronx spoke first. "I say we go public. Full transparency. Let the community know exactly who and what we're dealing with."

Bilal shook his head. "If we do that without a proper rollout, Kareem spins it. Says we're reactionary. Petty. Turns Isa into a misunderstood whistleblower."

"He's not a whistleblower," Bronx snapped. "He's a saboteur."

"Agreed," I said. "But we have to be strategic. The truth is only as powerful as the way it's delivered."

Bilal finally picked up the flash drive. Turned it in his palm like he was weighing the burden of it.

"We release this," he said, "we lose people. Not just Isa's followers. Fence-sitters. Folks who still believe in unity at any cost."

I leaned against the wall.

"Then maybe it's time we stop trying to save everyone."

Bronx nodded. "Better to move with a few who are clean than a crowd that's compromised."

Bilal sighed, heavy. "You planning to include this in your Ummah Report interview?"

I paused.

"I might."

"Then make sure you don't just expose the lie," he said. "Show them what the truth can be. Otherwise we're just building rubble."

That stuck.

Because he was right.

We weren't just burning bridges.

We were lighting torches.

And from now on, the only direction was forward.

The studio was colder than I expected.

Sterile. Bright. Clean lines and smooth silence. The kind of place built to make your words sound more important—or more dangerous.

The producer, Fariha, greeted me warmly. Hijab wrapped in deep olive, clipboard in hand. Her smile was kind, but her eyes were sharp. She reminded me of Soraya. Or maybe what Soraya would've been if she worked behind cameras instead of books.

"We'll run a 45-minute segment," she said. "Some pre-questions, but most will be live. You good with that?"

"Long as you don't clip me into a villain."

She smiled. "You tell your truth. I'll do the rest."

The lights came on.

The camera blinked.

And I took a breath.

The host introduced me gently—"Jibril Salaam: educator, community organizer, faith leader, father." The kind of intro that's flattering, but weighty. Then came the first real question.

"Your movement has faced setbacks. Fractures. Even internal betrayals. What's held it together?"

I looked into the camera.

Not at the audience.

At the people I owed something to.

"Service," I said. "And memory."

The host tilted her head. "Memory?"

I nodded. "We don't forget where we come from. We don't erase our mistakes. But we build forward—with those lessons as the blueprint."

Next question.

"There's been talk—evidence, even—that someone close to your inner circle was feeding intel to a rival initiative. Do you care to comment?"

This was it.

I could dodge.

Or I could define.

"We've confirmed betrayal," I said evenly. "A member of our team passed sensitive material to a former affiliate—someone known for exploiting movements more than building them."

I didn't name Isa.

But I didn't protect him either.

"We've responded internally. We're tightening our structure. More accountability. Less charisma, more character."

The host paused.

Then asked something I didn't expect.

"What would you say to that person now?"

I exhaled.

"I forgive you," I said. "But you're not coming back."

Silence.

Then—

"That's… clear," the host said, surprised.

"It has to be," I replied. "Because clarity is compassion. For our people. For the mission. For the future."

The interview aired on a Friday night.

By Saturday morning, my phone was a battleground—texts, voicemails, emails flooding in like a storm surge. Some congratulating. Some condemning. Others… just confused.

"Bro you really went there?"

"Finally—someone said it."

"You could've kept that in-house."

"You just gave him more fuel."

"Thank you. From all of us who've been too afraid to speak."

The community group chats lit up like bonfires.

One message thread split down the middle. Half affirming the transparency. The other half? Defending Isa's "intentions." Saying I'd gone too far. Said I'd shamed him without trial.

But it wasn't a trial.

It was a funeral.

A quiet one. For trust.

Rasheeda pulled me aside that afternoon while I was helping unload diapers at the shelter. Her tone wasn't angry—just surgical.

"You did the right thing," she said. "But don't expect applause for doing what leaders are supposed to do."

I nodded.

Bronx was less subtle.

"You drew the line. Now we'll see who steps across it."

Even Soraya called, her voice softer than usual.

"You said it clean," she told me. "Didn't name him. Didn't dance around it either. That's rare."

But not everyone was pleased.

A few sponsors pulled out. Not in protest—just in fear. Fear of controversy. Fear of headlines. Fear of standing next to a name that might attract heat.

And Isa?

He went silent.

No retaliation.

No denial.

Just… gone.

For now.

It was nearly midnight when I stepped into the nursery.

The room smelled like lavender lotion and old storybooks. One twin snored gently in the crib. The other gripped a toy car in his fist like he'd fallen asleep mid-battle. Imani's bedroom light was off, but I could hear the faint murmur of her nighttime du'a through the wall.

I stood there, in that quiet.

Not as an organizer.

Not as a spokesperson.

Just… a father.

A man trying to raise something solid in a world that wouldn't stop shaking.

I looked down at the twin closest to me. His curls were a mess. His pajama shirt was twisted. But his chest rose and fell like nothing outside that crib could ever touch him.

I envied that.

And I promised—right there, right then.

That I would not build this house of faith on borrowed bricks. That I would not raise leaders who inherited silence, or boys who thought trust was something to whisper about in corners.

I would teach them to stand.

Even when it hurt.

Even when it cost.

Especially when it cost.

Because revolutions were never about charisma.

They were about character.

And while betrayal had stolen our time, it had gifted us clarity.

We would move forward now.

Lean.

Limping.

But true.

Chapter Eighteen

The Quiet Storm

If you weren't paying attention, you'd miss her completely.

Soraya didn't demand a room—she earned it. Always the last to speak and the first to listen, she moved like someone who'd seen enough chaos to no longer be fascinated by it. She wasn't interested in building platforms for performance. She was busy building lifelines.

Lately, I'd been noticing her more. Not in that way—though anyone with a pulse and an eye for depth could admit she had a quiet beauty about her. But in a time when people were unraveling and ambition came dressed in deceit, Soraya remained unbothered and unshaken. She'd become something rare in these spaces: consistent.

It wasn't always like that.

Back in the early days, when the movement was still new and hungry, she'd been one of the first sisters to organize a strategy session that didn't involve shouting over men with fragile egos. She ran logistics for our women's outreach and could mobilize five masjids in a single afternoon. Still, no one gave her proper credit—especially the professor. He overlooked her contributions like so many others, calling her "the sister with the clipboard." That was his first mistake.

The second was underestimating her memory.

She'd been one of the earliest critics of the Black Up model—not because she opposed its vision, but because she understood it better than most. She was the one who flagged how the centralization of leadership would make us vulnerable. She was the one who insisted we develop a succession plan. Nobody listened.

And yet, Soraya never made it about ego. When the professor fell from grace, she didn't gloat. She simply stepped up.

We were sitting in a small community room one Thursday evening—just Soraya, myself, and a stack of poorly labeled donation receipts from three cities. I was trying to make sense of a spreadsheet that might as well have been in Latin. She was cross-referencing ledger entries without breaking a sweat.

"Do you ever sleep?" I muttered.

"Sleep is for the content," she replied dryly, still typing.

I looked up at her, and for the first time in a while, I noticed she wasn't just tired—she was grieving. I don't mean the loud, performative kind either. This was the grief of someone who had made peace with loss long before it arrived.

"You alright?"

She paused, fingers hovering over the keyboard. "I'm used to people walking away when they get uncomfortable. I just didn't think I'd have to do the same thing with a cause."

That hit.

"I know you were close to the old model," I offered gently.

She smiled, but it was the kind that doesn't reach the eyes. "No, I was close to the mission. The model was always shaky. We just couldn't admit it because we loved what it represented."

I nodded. We all did. Back then, the movement gave us purpose. Gave us language. Gave us belonging. Even if it came with cracks, it was still ours. That night, Soraya told me about her brother.

He'd died ten years ago, shot down outside a convenience store by police officers who said he "matched the description." He was unarmed, nineteen, and on his way to drop off some college applications. The story barely made local news.

"That's why I don't show up just to show up," she said. "That's why I don't do optics. I'm not here for a photo. I'm here because nobody was there for my family. I can't let that happen to someone else."

And just like that, I understood.

This wasn't just another resume-builder for her. This was the work.

Since then, I'd noticed that when tensions flared in our newer gatherings, Soraya was the one holding the middle. She bridged the younger sisters with the older aunties. She was organizing quarterly check-ins with Black Muslim therapists for our volunteers. She brought dignity back into our operations, one spreadsheet and healing circle at a time.

But not everyone was ready for her kind of leadership.

There were whispers now. Isa had planted doubts about her loyalty. Said she was "too independent" and "hard to collaborate with." Claimed she was going behind the group's back to form her own organization. I knew better. Isa's words reeked of control, and now that we had quietly demoted him to an advisory-only role, he was feeling the shift. Soraya didn't make power plays—she made structure. And men like Isa feared structure they couldn't control.

At our next meeting, when we reviewed the proposals for national expansion, it was Soraya's name at the top of three regional blueprints. Her fingerprints were all over the plans: budget caps, local partnerships, layered accountability.

She stood to speak, and the room fell silent—not out of command, but out of respect.

"I know we've been through a lot," she began. "And I know many of us are cautious about who we trust now. But I need you all to hear me when I say: this next phase can't look like the last one. We need less personality and more principles. We don't need saviors—we need systems."

I felt myself nodding. The rest of the room did too.

Later that night, I walked her out to her car.

"You're different now," I told her.

"Better or worse?"

"Both," I smirked. "But mostly better."

She chuckled and unlocked her door. "Jibril, I don't need you to protect me. I just need you to keep showing up."

"I can do that."

She hesitated before getting in. "There's something coming. I don't know what yet, but it's going to test all of us. Just be ready."

And with that, she was gone.

I stood in the parking lot a little longer than I planned, her words echoing in my chest.

We'd rebuilt something. Not perfect. Not polished. But real.

And for the first time in a long time, I believed we might actually be ready—if we listened to the quiet storm among us.

The next morning, the whispers began.

Not loud. Not accusatory. But persistent.

"Soraya's getting too much shine."

"Why she leading all the regional stuff?"

"Wasn't she just logistics last year?"

"You sure she's not building her own thing on the side?"

Bronx heard it first—from two younger brothers outside the masjid, speaking too freely by the wudu station. One of them tried to backpedal when he saw Bronx standing nearby. The other didn't even flinch.

"She just moves different," the kid said. "That type always got their own plan."

Bronx said nothing. He just looked at him long enough for silence to reclaim the air.

Later that day, he pulled me aside at the rec center.

"Watch your people," he said. "Jealousy don't always scream. Sometimes it whispers in the name of collaboration."

I knew what he meant.

The fear wasn't Soraya's ambition.

It was her competence.

She wasn't loud. She didn't beg for titles. She didn't network for clout.

She just did the work—and made it look effortless.

But some brothers only know how to respect power when it comes wrapped in ego.

And Soraya didn't come wrapped in anything but results.

I found Bilal in the back of the masjid after Isha, scrolling through his phone like he was trying to find a reason to stay present. He didn't look up until I sat beside him.

"You good?" I asked.

"Define good," he said, still looking at the screen.

I let the silence stretch between us. Bilal wasn't the type to be pried open. He opened on his own terms—or not at all.

"People are talking," I finally said. "Not about you. About Soraya."

He nodded once. "Of course they are."

"She's rising fast."

"She's been rising," he said sharply. "Y'all just started watching."

That caught me off guard. I turned toward him fully.

"What does that mean?"

He locked his phone and finally looked at me. "It means some of us been building trenches while others were out chasing headlines. She's steady. She's sharp. And yeah, maybe she scares people who got used to leading without being led."

"You think I'm scared of her?"

He didn't blink. "I think you're scared of losing control. Of being part of something you didn't personally design."

I wanted to argue. Wanted to explain. But I didn't.

Because part of me knew he was right.

"She's not trying to take over," I said softly. "She's trying to stabilize what we almost lost."

Bilal leaned back against the wall.

"I respect her," he said. "But respect don't erase dynamics. If you want her to lead, say that. If you want us to follow, then stop acting like it's a group vote when it's already a coronation."

I didn't have a clever comeback.

Just sat there, wondering when the circle stopped feeling like a circle—and started feeling like a tug-of-war.

The email came on a Tuesday.

Soraya was sipping tea in the multipurpose room, finalizing logistics for the fall mentorship pilot when she opened it. The subject line was vague: "Strategic Opportunity – Private Inquiry."

Inside was an invitation.

A well-established foundation—progressive, well-funded, quietly influential—wanted to support her directly. No intermediaries. No committee votes. No brotherhood consensus.

"We've been following your leadership trajectory," the message read, "and believe your vision for Black Muslim women's intellectual and spiritual development deserves its own platform. We're prepared to provide a seed grant to launch a regional network—women-led, women-governed. Fully autonomous."

It was flattering.

But also a trap.

She didn't say anything at first.

She went to the masjid. Prayed. Sat with her Quran. Then she called Rasheeda.

"I don't know what to do," she said. "This could help so many sisters… but it'll look like I'm going rogue."

Rasheeda didn't hesitate. "Then don't move in silence. Bring it to the group."

"They won't see it as an opportunity. They'll see it as division."

Rasheeda lowered her voice. "Then make sure they know your intention before they hear your decision."

That night, Soraya called me.

"I got an offer," she said plainly. "It's real money. Real autonomy."

I stayed quiet, letting her speak.

"I'm not trying to split off," she continued. "But I won't keep apologizing for growing, either."

"You don't have to apologize," I said.

"But I do have to decide."

And I knew—whatever she chose next would shift everything.

Not because of power.

But because of principle.

We met in the upstairs classroom of the old community center. No microphones. No livestreams. Just dry erase markers, uncomfortable chairs, and truth.

Soraya stood at the front, palms open. Calm. Honest.

"I received a grant offer," she said. "It's real. It's specific. And it's for me—not for us."

A few eyebrows raised. Bilal leaned back. Bronx crossed his arms. Ameer looked from side to side like someone had just passed gas in the masjid.

"They want me to launch a women-led, autonomous satellite. Full funding. Full freedom. I didn't ask for it—but I won't lie. It aligns with a lot of what I've been working toward."

She paused, looking at each face.

"I'm telling you because I respect you. Because I need you to know this isn't a betrayal—it's a choice. One I haven't made yet. But one I'm prepared to make."

Bronx shifted in his seat. "Why not just bring it under our banner?"

"Because the sisters have been asking for space we haven't created," she said. "Not just permission to speak—but a mandate to lead."

It was quiet for a long time.

Then Rasheeda—who wasn't even supposed to be in the room—spoke from the back.

"What if it didn't have to be either-or?"

All heads turned.

She walked forward calmly, carrying a legal pad filled with notes.

"What if we create a leadership council—not advisory, not honorary. Equal votes. Shared decisions. Half men, half women. Operational autonomy where needed. Strategic unity where it counts."

Soraya blinked.

"I'm not asking to run everything," Rasheeda continued. "I'm asking us to finally stop pretending that leadership only wears one face."

The air changed.

Bilal cleared his throat. "You proposing co-leadership?"

"I'm proposing survival," she said. "We've already seen what happens when one man controls the mic."

I looked at Soraya. She looked at me.

And for the first time in months, we nodded—together.

It was Ameer who opened the door.

He had invited them.

Three young organizers—two sisters, one brother—all in their early twenties, all born into a post-9/11, post-Obama, post-everything era. Raised in a time when activism lived on both the streets and the algorithm. They'd come dressed in hoodies, Doc Martens, and conviction.

At first, the room shifted uncomfortably. Bronx squinted. Bilal frowned. Even I felt myself tense up.

But Soraya stood and greeted them warmly, offering chairs.

"I thought this was a leadership meeting," one of the sisters said with a hint of challenge. "And if we're talking about the future… we're already here."

No one argued.

Ameer introduced them quickly—Jamila, Rashad, and Noor. All under 25. All actively building youth programming in the shadow of our work—but with their own language. Their own rhythm.

"We respect what y'all have done," Jamila began. "Seriously. But we also need to say this: If leadership doesn't evolve, we'll build without it."

Rashad added, "Too many of our friends see the movement as nostalgia. Not power. You can't just slap a new name on an old model and expect it to reach us."

Noor finished it off. "We need leadership that mentors us, not manages us. That invites questions, not just applause."

It wasn't rebellion.

It was a warning.

And they weren't wrong.

Soraya looked over at me. Her eyes said it before her lips did:

"This is who we're building for."

Bronx and I walked in silence down the sidewalk behind the community center.

The air was heavy with Houston heat and unspoken truths. Streetlights flickered overhead. A dog barked somewhere in the distance. It was one of those nights where everything felt like a metaphor.

"You remember when this was all about flyers and flyers?" Bronx asked, hands in his pockets.

I smirked. "Flyers and feelings."

He nodded. "Now it's spreadsheets and therapy groups. And sisters who don't wait to be invited."

I glanced over. "That a problem?"

"No," he said, slowing his pace. "It's growth. But growth feels like grief sometimes. Like saying goodbye to the version of us we fought so hard to become."

I knew what he meant.

We were no longer the hungry idealists storming the mall with chants and duct-taped banners. We were men now—tired, thoughtful, surrounded by people smarter than us, holier than us, more prepared than we had been.

"You think we're being replaced?" I asked.

He shook his head. "I think we're being humbled. And that's harder."

We walked a little longer.

Then he stopped and looked me dead in the eye.

"Let her lead, bro."

"Soraya?"

He nodded. "She's not asking to take over. She's asking to take care. Let her."

I swallowed that slowly.

"Don't be the brother who clings to the mic just because he learned how to use it first."

That one hit hard.

Because Bronx had never told me to step back.

Until now.

Sara was sitting cross-legged on the floor, surrounded by coloring books and unfolded laundry. One twin was asleep on her lap. The other was using a toy masjid as a race track. She looked up as I entered, reading me in a glance.

"Rough night?" she asked.

"Truthful night," I said, kicking off my shoes.

She patted the carpet beside her. I sank into it like a man returning to earth.

"You ever feel like this thing's passing us by?" I asked.

She tilted her head. "This thing? Or your version of it?"

I laughed. Softly. "Fair."

She waited. Patient. That's how she always loved me—without pushing, just making space for my words to arrive.

"We're talking about a new leadership structure," I said. "Half men. Half women. Shared decision-making. Soraya would co-lead."

"And you?" she asked.

"I'd still lead. But not… alone."

She smiled—not with surprise, but recognition.

"That's what you prayed for, Jibril. Not more power. More protection. More accountability. You've been carrying this alone longer than you admit."

I leaned back against the couch. "It just feels like… if I step back, people might think I failed."

She touched my arm.

"Let them think what they want. The only people who matter are the ones watching you raise these babies. And they'll remember how you led together."

I closed my eyes, letting her words settle.

Sara never needed a pulpit.

But she preached the kind of sermons that stayed with you forever.

The leadership council was finalized the following Sunday.

Nine seats.

Four brothers.

Four sisters.

One rotating chair for youth representation—elected every quarter.

It didn't happen with a press release or a celebratory photo. There were no hashtags. No banners. Just a simple gathering in the masjid library. Folded chairs. A whiteboard. And intention.

Soraya co-chaired.

So did I.

Bilal agreed to oversee policy. Rasheeda took on wellness. Ameer handled community outreach. Bronx, ever the reluctant warrior, volunteered to mentor new male leaders through conflict resolution.

The room felt… right.

Not perfect.

But balanced.

For once, it didn't feel like we were performing leadership.

We were practicing it.

I looked around at the circle—at Jamila, the youth rep, scribbling notes furiously. At Soraya calmly guiding the agenda. At the brothers listening without interrupting.

And something in me finally unclenched.

Not because we had solved everything.

But because we had finally learned to share the solving.

Afterward, as people packed up, Soraya lingered.

She didn't say much. Just looked at me and asked, "You ready for this?"

I smiled. "I was born in the storm. But this—this is peace."

She nodded, turning toward the door.

I watched her walk away—not as a subordinate, not as a rival.

But as a partner.

And as the last light flickered off in the hallway, I realized something:

The revolution I feared losing wasn't over.

It had just grown up.

Chapter Nineteen

The Soraya Situation

Soraya had a gift for showing up when things were just starting to settle down—like a perfectly timed plot twist in a movie you didn't realize you were starring in.

She called out of the blue on a Monday morning, her voice syrupy sweet but threaded with urgency. "I'm in town. Just for a few days. Let's grab coffee?"

Coffee, of course. The universal code for, "I have something dramatic to share but I'm pretending it's casual."

I agreed—reluctantly, out of a mix of curiosity and that indefinable energy she carried. She was unpredictable, magnetic, and exhausting in the most elegant way. We met at a café that tried too hard to look Parisian. I wore my neutral face, the one that pretends nothing ever gets under my skin.

She arrived wearing a burnt orange hijab and oversized sunglasses that made her look like she stepped out of a Vogue editorial about mysterious women with complicated pasts. She waved like we were old friends who'd simply lost touch, not co-conspirators in an emotional minefield.

"So," she said, sitting down without removing her glasses. "I'm getting married."

I blinked. "To who? And why do I feel like I'm the last to know?"

She smiled as if I'd handed her the line she'd been waiting for. "It's not official yet. But it's serious. And I need your help."

I waited. With Soraya, the help she needed could range from assembling IKEA furniture to negotiating peace treaties between exes.

"It's Bilal's cousin."

I nearly choked on my coffee. "You mean the cousin who tried to sell protein shakes at Rasheeda's birthday dinner?"

She nodded like this made perfect sense. "Yes, but he's grown. And passionate. He's helping me with a non-profit startup focused on Muslim women's mental health. We're building something real, Jibril."

That was Soraya in a nutshell: equal parts chaos and conviction. She could make a pyramid scheme sound like a divine calling.

"I support it," I said cautiously. "But why do you need my help?"

She leaned forward, finally removing her sunglasses. Her eyes held a storm—regret, determination, and something like mischief.

"I want you to talk to Bronx."

Now I was confused. "What does Bronx have to do with this?"

"He's been weird since I started working with Bilal's cousin. Real protective. Like he knows something I don't. I just need you to clear the air. You're like a father to both of us, right?"

That word—father—hit differently coming from Soraya. She had a way of attaching emotional weight to everyday conversation like it was a contact sport. I agreed, mostly out of obligation, but also because I didn't want her calling someone else with a plan even more outrageous.

Later that week, I called Bronx and arranged a meetup at the gym. He came with his usual gruff demeanor but wore a new hoodie that said "Don't Talk to Me While I'm Resting," which felt aggressively on-brand.

We benched a few sets before I brought it up. "You got a problem with Soraya and this cousin?"

He wiped his forehead with a towel. "Not exactly."

"That's not a no."

He sighed. "Look, I just don't like the guy. Something about him don't sit right. He's got shiny-shoe energy."

"Shiny-shoe energy?"

"Yeah, like… he moisturizes his knuckles. I don't trust him."

That was Bronx logic in a nutshell.

"You think Soraya's making a mistake?" I asked.

"I think Soraya makes decisions like she's speed dating fate."

I had to stifle a laugh. "So what do you want me to do? Stop her?"

"No," he said. "Just… talk to her. See where her head's at. And maybe remind her she's not indestructible."

I did. Soraya and I met again a few days later, this time at a community center she was helping remodel. She wore paint-splattered jeans and had a drill clipped to her belt like a symbol of independence.

"Bronx thinks your fiancé uses too much lotion," I said bluntly.

She laughed—loud and unfiltered. "That man once owned three pairs of the same black hoodie. He's not exactly my style guide."

"But you care what he thinks."

She grew quiet. "I care that he cares. But I'm tired of living in his shadow."

There it was. The real Soraya. Beneath the flair, the sunglasses, the sarcasm, there was always a wounded clarity.

"I'm not saying don't live your life," I said gently. "I'm saying make sure you're choosing peace, not just change."

She nodded, swallowing emotion that hovered behind her usual bravado. "Maybe I needed you to say that."

I left the center unsure of what would come next. Soraya's life was a whirlwind. But I knew one thing for sure—she was about to shake up everything.

And something told me, in that strange, sixth-sense way I trusted more than logic, that her story wasn't just a subplot anymore.

She was about to change the whole narrative.

Two days after our talk, Bronx sent me a text:

"She's grown. I get that. But I ain't clapping for the wrong dude just to keep the peace."

I called him, but he didn't pick up.

That's how Bronx did emotions—through silence and skipped reps. But it wasn't just about Soraya's fiancé. It was something deeper.

Later that week, I found him hitting the heavy bag at the gym—no gloves, just tape and fury. I watched for a few minutes before speaking.

"You gonna break your wrist."

He didn't stop swinging.

"Better my wrist than my trust."

I leaned against the wall. "This about her or about being left behind?"

That made him stop.

He turned slowly, breathing hard. "It's about people thinking loyalty is a phase."

There it was.

Bronx wasn't jealous. He was protective. Of her. Of the mission. Of what they had built side by side—before the titles, the donors, the flyers with Soraya's name in bold.

"She's not replacing you," I said.

He unwrapped his hand slowly. "She already did. Just didn't tell me."

Bilal showed up to the masjid brunch late, wearing a kufi that looked like it had been ironed five minutes ago and eyes that hadn't slept in two days.

I pulled him aside after the du'a, away from the noise of kids and half-drunk coffee cups.

"You heard about Soraya?"

He didn't look surprised. "Everybody's heard about Soraya. The woman could announce a shoe sale and it'd make the WhatsApp circuit in ten minutes."

"So?"

He smirked. "So what?"

"What do you think?"

He shrugged. "I think she's smart. Strategic. Maybe too strategic."

I gave him the side-eye. "You think she's playing this?"

"I think women like Soraya don't just fall into relationships. They select them—like a chess piece. She didn't trip into this. She's placing herself."

I waited.

"But I also think…" He stopped, scanning the room. Then sighed. "I think I envy her."

That caught me off guard.

"I've been stuck in the same gear since my divorce," he admitted. "Still leading. Still pushing. But no softness. No partnership. Just… direction."

I sat with that.

We never talked about Bilal's loneliness. Not really.

"I used to think love was a reward," he said. "You build, you sacrifice, you get peace in return. But now? Now I think some of us were born to serve and die tired."

He sipped from his water bottle like that was the end of the sentence.

But it wasn't.

"I don't know if Soraya's making the right choice," he added. "But I know she's choosing. And that counts for something."

Rasheeda found me in the kitchen after the leadership check-in, where I'd been hiding with a lukewarm plate of samosas and a plastic fork that had lost a tine.

"You got a minute?" she asked, arms crossed.

When Rasheeda asks that, she's not asking.

"Always," I said, bracing myself.

She closed the door behind us. No drama. Just clarity.

"I've been watching the way y'all talk about Soraya," she said. "And I've been watching the way you don't talk about what's really bothering you."

I raised an eyebrow. "What's that supposed to mean?"

"It means men like you and Bronx have always done well with strong women—until those women stop orbiting you."

That landed heavier than I expected.

"You think this is about control?"

"I think it's about discomfort. Soraya's not asking for permission. She's building in real time. And instead of backing her, some of y'all are waiting to see if she falls."

I didn't respond. Not because I disagreed. But because I knew she was right.

"She's not perfect," Rasheeda added. "But neither are the brothers she's been cleaning up after for the last two years."

Then came the real line.

"If Soraya fails, it won't be because she couldn't lead. It'll be because the men who claimed to believe in her were too busy nursing egos to carry bricks."

That was Rasheeda.

The most gentle fire you'd ever walk through barefoot.

Rasheeda found me in the kitchen after the leadership check-in, where I'd been hiding with a lukewarm plate of samosas and a plastic fork that had lost a tine.

"You got a minute?" she asked, arms crossed.

When Rasheeda asks that, she's not asking.

"Always," I said, bracing myself.

She closed the door behind us. No drama. Just clarity.

"I've been watching the way y'all talk about Soraya," she said. "And I've been watching the way you don't talk about what's really bothering you."

I raised an eyebrow. "What's that supposed to mean?"

"It means men like you and Bronx have always done well with strong women—until those women stop orbiting you."

That landed heavier than I expected.

"You think this is about control?"

"I think it's about discomfort. Soraya's not asking for permission. She's building in real time. And instead of backing her, some of y'all are waiting to see if she falls."

I didn't respond. Not because I disagreed. But because I knew she was right.

"She's not perfect," Rasheeda added. "But neither are the brothers she's been cleaning up after for the last two years."

Then came the real line.

"If Soraya fails, it won't be because she couldn't lead. It'll be because the men who claimed to believe in her were too busy nursing egos to carry bricks."

That was Rasheeda.

The most gentle fire you'd ever walk through barefoot.

The invite came late Wednesday night.

Soraya texted me:

"Big panel next weekend. National spotlight. They want me to close it out."

I responded:

"That's big. You ready?"

She replied:

"More than ready. But I want you to introduce me."

I stared at the screen for a long time.

It wasn't that I didn't want to. It was that I knew what it meant.

This wasn't just an intro. It was a passing of the mic.

It was a public declaration that this sister—this strategist, this visionary, this storm wrapped in silk and spreadsheets—was no longer emerging.

She had arrived.

I called her the next morning.

"You sure?" I asked.

"I wouldn't ask if I wasn't," she said. "But if it's too much—if you're not ready—say that. Don't say yes just to be polite."

I chuckled. "You don't ask for things. You assign them."

She didn't laugh.

"I'm serious, Jibril," she said. "This is important. And not just for me. For every girl sitting in the audience who needs to see a man lift a woman without claiming credit for her flight."

That hit.

Hard.

"Say less," I said. "I'll write something that matters."

And I did.

The following week, in a packed auditorium, I walked onto that stage.

Looked out into a crowd full of hijabs, kufis, natural curls, suits, sneakers, and soul.

Then I spoke into the mic—not as a gatekeeper, not as a mentor, but as a witness.

"To introduce this next speaker," I said, "is not to endorse her. It is to affirm her. Her leadership didn't start today. It started the first time she chose principle over popularity. The first time she built behind the scenes while others fought for the spotlight."

I paused.

"She doesn't ask for applause. She asks for action. And if we're wise, we'll give her both."

When Soraya stepped out, the applause rose before she said a single word.

And for the first time in a long time, I didn't feel eclipsed.

I felt proud.

Bronx missed the panel.

Didn't call. Didn't text. Didn't post. Just vanished.

I didn't take it personal—at first. Bronx had always moved like a drumbeat only he could hear. But after two days with no word, something didn't sit right.

I found him on the far end of MacGregor Park, sitting on a broken bench near the old basketball courts. Hoodie up. Elbows on knees. Face buried in his palms.

He didn't flinch when I walked up.

"You good?" I asked, already knowing the answer.

"Define good," he said without looking up.

That was twice in one month I'd heard that line.

I sat down beside him. The wind moved through the trees like a slow exhale.

"She did good," I said. "Killed it, actually."

"I know," he muttered.

"She asked about you."

"I figured."

Silence stretched between us like old gum on hot pavement.

Then he said it.

"I feel like I'm watching the house we built turn into a museum I can't afford tickets to."

That landed deep.

He looked at me, eyes tired.

"She's leading. You're adapting. Even Bilal's got his second wind. And me? I'm just… heavy."

I didn't speak. Just listened.

"I gave everything to this," he continued. "My marriage. My peace. My damn body. And now I'm sitting here wondering if I'm still needed—or just nostalgic."

I reached into my coat pocket and handed him a folded piece of paper. A flyer Soraya had printed weeks ago. On it: a youth program proposal. At the bottom—under mentorship leads—was one name: Brother Bronx.

"She still sees you," I said.

He stared at it.

"I don't need to lead," he said. "I just don't want to be left behind."

"You're not," I said. "You're part of the foundation. And no matter how high the building goes, the foundation stays beneath it all."

That was the first time in a while I saw Bronx breathe easy.

Isa showed up unannounced.

Friday. Right after maghrib. I was stacking chairs in the masjid multipurpose room when the door creaked open and there he was—dressed sharp, as always, with that carefully curated smile that had charmed half the city and infuriated the other half.

"Jibril," he said quietly.

I nodded, unsure whether to shake his hand or call security.

"I'm not here to defend myself," he added quickly. "Just to say something. And then I'll leave."

I folded my arms and let him speak.

"I was wrong," he said. "I played both sides. Tried to secure influence while pretending to serve something bigger. That's on me."

He paused. Looked around the empty room.

"This place… it's still yours. Still hers. Still theirs. It was never mine to leverage. I see that now."

I didn't soften. Not yet.

"You hurt people," I said. "You betrayed a movement you helped build."

"I know."

"Why now?"

"Because silence is a type of arrogance. And I've been arrogant long enough."

That stung. Because I remembered being that kind of man once, too.

"I'm leaving the city," Isa said. "Taking a job overseas. Academic work. Consultancy. It's quieter. Better for someone like me."

I nodded once. "Closure?"

"Maybe just consequence."

He reached into his coat pocket and pulled out a flash drive.

"Everything I have. Emails. Contacts. Internal documents. Funding traces. Yours now."

I took it reluctantly.

"Good luck, Jibril," he said, turning to leave.

Then paused.

"And tell Soraya… she was always right."

She asked to meet at the garden behind the community center.

No fanfare. No witnesses. Just gravel paths and string lights that buzzed quietly above.

Soraya was wearing navy again—her signature—and no makeup. She looked calm, the kind of calm you earn after walking through every kind of fire and still choosing to plant flowers.

"You came," she said, offering a soft smile.

"Wouldn't miss it."

She handed me a folded note. "I wrote this for tomorrow. If you're still okay being the one to read it at the ceremony."

I tucked it into my jacket without opening it. "I trust your words."

She sat on the edge of a planter bed and looked up at the lights.

"I used to imagine something different," she said. "Bigger. Louder. Maybe even a little messier. But now? I just want peace. Quiet mornings. Honest work. A home that doesn't require rebuilding every three months."

I nodded. "You deserve that."

She glanced over at me.

"Do you think I chose wrong?"

"Not my question to answer," I said. "But I think you chose intentionally. That's more than most people ever do."

We sat in silence for a while. Not awkward. Just full.

Then she asked, "Did you ever wonder—about us?"

I didn't lie.

"Sometimes. But it always felt… incomplete. Like we were the same book, just written in different fonts."

She laughed gently. "That's poetic. And probably true."

She stood and faced me fully.

"Thank you," she said. "Not for the work. For the witnessing. You always saw me. Even when it made you uncomfortable."

I swallowed hard.

"I always will."

We didn't hug. Didn't linger.

Just a nod.

And then she walked away, heels crunching over gravel, back straight, spirit intact.

She wasn't a chapter in someone else's story anymore.

She was the author now.

The room was packed.

Not with press, not with clout chasers—just people. Aunties in embroidered abayas. Youth volunteers in Jordans. Elders with canes and quiet memories. The whole room buzzed with the kind of sacred expectancy you can't choreograph.

The imam kept it short. The contract was signed. Her fiancé—Bilal's cousin, still moisturized and oddly charming—stood beside her with a nervous smile and a posture that said he knew he was marrying someone far more prepared for life than he'd ever be.

I was asked to say a few words.

I pulled Soraya's note from my jacket, unfolded it slowly, and read aloud:

"To build something that lasts, you need more than plans and patience.

You need people who are willing to stand in the gap between what is and what should be.

You need faith that isn't performative.

You need brothers who know when to lead—and when to follow.

And you need sisters who stop waiting to be invited and start building their own tables.

Today isn't the end of my journey.

It's just a new season.

And if you ever forget why we started, look around this room.

This is what we were fighting for."

I looked up from the page.

She stood beside her new husband, not radiant—but rooted. Not glowing—but grounded.

And for the first time in years, I felt it—deep, warm, and complete:

We hadn't lost her.

We had launched her.

And the story she was writing now?

It didn't need our protection.

It just needed our blessing.

Chapter Twenty

The Reckoning and the Rise

The house was quiet.

Too quiet.

It was the kind of stillness you only get in the early morning, when the rest of the world is still deciding whether it wants to exist. I sat alone at the dining table with a cup of lukewarm tea, the kind Sara always made with too much honey. The twins had finally gone down. Imani was still asleep in her rainbow pajamas, half-tucked into a pile of picture books she never quite finished reading. Sara was in the other room prepping for her online halaqa with the new reverts—sisters from all over the country who now logged in weekly to hear her explain tawheed through the lens of trauma recovery and parenting toddlers.

And me?

I was sitting in the center of a life I wasn't sure I was qualified to lead anymore.

The movement was gaining momentum again. That should've felt good. We were back to doing real work—launching programs, partnering with clinics, holding neighborhood forums that actually made people feel heard. But something about it all felt… different. Heavier.

Maybe it was age. Or fatigue. Or maybe it was the quiet suspicion that this new season required a version of me I hadn't fully become yet.

The pressure of leadership is strange. People see the microphone and the sound bites, the prayer before the protest, the hugs after the meetings. They don't see the nights you stay awake, staring at a wall, wondering if the decisions you made today will ruin someone's tomorrow. They don't see the phone calls you ignore because you're afraid of what the voice on the other end might ask you to fix. They don't see how hard it is to be a "pillar" when all you want to do is crumble in peace.

There's a difference between being needed and being known. Lately, I wasn't sure which one I was anymore.

I thought about my daughters—tiny, loud, brilliant creatures who asked more questions than the Qur'an offered answers. I thought about Imani, watching me with wide eyes when I left the house with my kufi and laptop bag. What did she see? A leader? A martyr? A man who was always leaving but never gone long enough to miss?

Then I thought about the men.

Bronx. Bilal. Isa. Even the Professor.

Each of them had taught me something, broken something in me, or forced me to name a part of myself I didn't want to acknowledge.

And then, of course, there was Soraya.

The only person in the movement who could check me without bruising my ego. The only one who could pull a budget from a war zone and still have enough emotional bandwidth left to ask how my mother was doing. I'd fought beside warriors. I'd mourned with leaders. But Soraya? She sustained things. That kind of energy was rare. And terrifying.

The worst part of this calling—the thing no one tells you when they hand you a mic or put your name on a flyer—is that you spend half your time being everything to everyone, and the other half wondering who you are when the crowd disappears.

I stared at the letter again.

Not because I didn't believe it was from him—I knew that handwriting like I knew my own signature—but because I was trying to read what wasn't written. The tone was clipped. Strategic. Every word chosen like a chess move. It wasn't an invitation. It was a warning. Or maybe… a final test.

The old mosque where we started—he'd chosen that place on purpose.

Back then, we used to meet in the basement. Five brothers. One folding table. Notebooks with dreams too big for the margins. We weren't polished. We weren't organized. But we were hungry. We had fire in our bones and something to prove—to the community, to the country, to ourselves. I remember the Professor pacing like a general before battle, quoting Baldwin and Shabazz like they were both his uncles.

"You don't build movements," he said once, slamming his hand on the table. "You birth them. And if you don't scream, bleed, and pray through it, you're not doing it right."

We believed him.

We followed him.

And then we paid for it.

When everything collapsed—when the funding dried up, when the lawsuits started, when Bronx nearly lost his life—he disappeared. Ghosted. Not even a farewell khutbah or cryptic voice memo. Just gone. We spent years digging out of that crater.

Now here he was, slipping back into the frame with a note that smelled like unfinished business.

I didn't tell anyone I was going.

Not Sara. Not Rasheeda. Not even Bronx.

I packed light—flashlight, prayer rug, a small notebook, and one of the tasbih strings the Professor gave me years ago after a particularly brutal community organizing session. "You're gonna need this," he said. "Not for show—for survival."

The beads were chipped now, the string frayed, but I kept it.

I left the house just before eleven, telling Sara I had "some late paperwork" to review at the community office. She didn't ask questions, but she watched me closely—her eyes tracing me like she was memorizing the moment.

"Don't carry it all alone," she said softly.

Too late for that.

The city streets were nearly empty as I drove, the night air thick with summer stillness and something else—anticipation. Regret. Fear.

The mosque stood like a shadow of itself, boarded-up windows and rusted gates marking time. I parked across the street and stared for a while, wondering how many ghosts still lived inside. How many voices had once echoed through those walls with plans too bold for the world they were born into.

I crossed the street slowly. No lights. No cameras. Just me and the ache in my chest.

He was already there.

Waiting.

He was sitting on the old wudu bench near the back entrance, the same one we used to lean against after fajr, solving the world's problems before the sun was fully up.

Same coat.

Same kufi.

Same eyes.

But everything else about him was… smaller.

Not physically. Spiritually. He looked like a man who had once wrestled nations and was now just trying to sleep through the night without his past knocking on the walls of his conscience.

"I wasn't sure you'd come," he said.

"I wasn't sure you deserved it."

He nodded, like he'd expected the punch and accepted it.

"I didn't ask for forgiveness," he said.

"Good. Because I didn't bring any."

The air between us cracked open. Not with noise. With truth. Thick and heavy and shaped like history.

He reached into his coat and pulled out a small black flash drive. "Everything," he said, holding it out. "Donor records. Internal memos. Contacts. Surveillance logs. Even the communications with Isa. All of it."

I didn't take it.

Not yet.

"You think this makes it right?"

"No," he said plainly. "But it makes it known."

I finally took it. Cold in my hand. Heavy.

He looked at me for a long time, like a man staring into a mirror he didn't quite recognize anymore.

"You remind me of how I used to sound," he said. "Before I started playing politics with purpose."

I didn't respond. Didn't need to.

"I was wrong," he added. "About the structure. About centralizing power. About making myself the symbol instead of the servant."

That got my attention.

"You finally see it now?"

"I saw it then. I just didn't care. And by the time I did, I was too far in."

We sat in silence, side by side now, like two tired veterans swapping war stories that no one else would understand.

"Why now?" I asked.

"Because you're building again. And this time… it looks different. It looks like what we meant to do."

He stood slowly. His knees cracked like old wood.

"You've got a chance to fix it," he said. "Don't waste it trying to prove anything to ghosts like me."

He walked off into the night, no dramatic exit, no final speech.

Just a shadow fading into deeper shadows.

And for the first time, I didn't hate him.

I just felt sorry for him.

The house was asleep when I got home.

I slipped off my shoes and stepped through the dark, each floorboard creak sounding like a question I couldn't yet answer. The flash drive was still in my pocket, but it felt like it had its own pulse. A living thing. Full of secrets, schemes, and sins.

I didn't go to bed.

I went out to the balcony.

Houston's night air had a way of making you feel both insignificant and deeply seen. The sky didn't judge you—it just held your failures next to its stars and dared you to find your place again.

I sat there for what felt like hours. Long enough for guilt to arrive, and long enough for peace to refuse to follow.

Sara joined me.

She always did, eventually.

She wrapped herself in a shawl and leaned against the doorframe. Didn't say a word at first—just watched me. She was good at that. Reading the silences between my sighs. Waiting for me to name the weight before she tried to lift it.

"He's back," I finally said.

Her eyes didn't blink.

"I figured," she replied. "Your spirit's been heavy all week."

I handed her the flash drive.

She held it like a live wire. "What's on it?"

"Everything. Enough to rebuild. Enough to destroy."

"And what are you going to do with it?"

That was the question, wasn't it?

Burn the old blueprint and start from scratch?

Or salvage what was good and dare to redeem what once betrayed us?

"I don't know," I admitted. "Part of me wants to throw it in the bayou and never look back."

"But?"

"But the movement isn't just about us anymore. It's about the kids at that charter school who stopped being suspended because we showed up. It's about the single mother who got a job through our network. The elder who found faith again because someone knocked on his door with groceries and a Qur'an."

She nodded. "So it's bigger than forgiveness now."

"It always was."

She walked over, took the flash drive, and placed it gently on the table next to the Qur'an.

Then she kissed my forehead.

"Then lead," she whispered. "And don't forget—Allah writes the real blueprint. You're just laying the bricks."

We met at the gym. Not because it was the most professional space, but because it was neutral ground. And sometimes, to talk about war, you needed a place built on sweat, struggle, and second chances.

Bronx rolled in first, hoodie up, face set. He hadn't said much since the incident with Soraya's engagement drama, but the fire behind his eyes told me he was ready for whatever this night would bring.

Bilal came next, sharp as ever. He carried a notebook, a thermos, and the familiar posture of a man who knew he'd have to talk less and listen more tonight.

Soraya arrived with purpose. No pretense. No smiles. Just a messenger bag and that look of someone who had already considered every possible outcome and showed up anyway.

Isa walked in last. No sunglasses this time. Just a plain black turtleneck and the air of a man who knew he was still on probation.

Rasheeda took her seat beside me without fanfare. She didn't speak unless she needed to, but when she did, rooms shifted.

We all sat in a circle, mismatched folding chairs arranged under the flickering gym lights. I placed the flash drive in the center like a loaded weapon.

"That's from him?" Bilal asked.

I nodded. "Everything. Full archive. No edits."

Silence.

Soraya leaned in. "So what's the move?"

I looked around the circle—my family, my tribe, my headache.

"We've spent the last two years trying to rebuild something that nearly killed us," I said. "And now, the very man who almost took it all has handed us the blueprint to either do it right… or walk away for good."

Bronx grunted. "I vote walk."

"Why?" Soraya asked.

"Because anything he touched is cursed. We try to use that data, that funding map, that infrastructure, and we're playing his game. We're feeding a ghost."

Isa cleared his throat. "With all due respect, ghosts have maps too. And sometimes, we need them."

Rasheeda tilted her head. "But at what cost? You want us to keep building on shaky ground because it's faster?"

"No," Isa said, calmer now. "I want us to be smarter than we were before."

Bilal tapped the notebook. "I've already drafted a new governance model. One with distributed leadership. Rotating board seats. Sisters included. No one person can be the face again. We can build this right."

Everyone looked at Soraya.

She took a breath. "If we use his blueprint, we vet every line. We rebuild it like survivors, not like disciples. We don't use it to resurrect him. We use it to ensure nobody like him rises again."

I nodded. "Then it's settled?"

A slow wave of agreement passed through the room. Not loud. Not unanimous. But real.

We weren't just moving forward.

We were re-authoring the story.

The decision was made, but the rollout had to be careful.

We weren't trying to make noise—we were trying to make sense. The community didn't need another brand. They needed stability. We weren't interested in performance anymore. We wanted process.

We called it the Justice Reimagined Initiative—a mouthful, maybe. But that was the point. No charisma-fueled acronym. No messiah complex baked into the logo. Just work. Just principle.

We didn't post a flashy flyer.

We released a letter. Handwritten. Signed by all of us.

It read:

"We come to you not with promises, but with presence.

We come not as leaders, but as servants.

We come to reimagine justice—not as a system we fight against, but as a life we live alongside you.

We got it wrong before.

This time, we're building with our eyes open."_

We attached a schedule of public forums. Real ones. No stages. Just circles. No VIPs. Just chairs.

We hosted the first in the community center gym, with plastic water bottles, boxed chicken wraps, and a single mic that kept cutting out.

But it didn't matter.

Over 120 people came. Black Muslim mothers. Teens in kufis and hoodies. Former critics. Recovering activists. Even a few uncles who once labeled us "those misguided kids who think justice is a brand."

We let them speak first.

A sister named Ummi Fatimah stood and said, "I came here to see if y'all were really ready to listen. Because I buried two sons to this system. And I'm tired of polished answers that don't hold my grief."

We didn't interrupt.

We just wrote down every word.

Then a college student, barely old enough to rent a car, raised his hand.

"I'm not looking for saviors," he said. "But I am looking for teachers. For models. For men who look like me and didn't lose themselves trying to be accepted."

Bronx stood. "Then we owe you that. All of us. Starting now."

Something shifted in the room after that. Not trust, not yet—but a softening.

People didn't want slogans. They wanted sight.

And we were finally starting to see.

At the end of the night, we didn't take a group photo.

We mopped the floors. Picked up trash. Sat with elders in folding chairs for another hour.

And that felt more like revolution than anything I'd ever done with a bullhorn.

Three days later, the email came.

It wasn't from the press. Not from an activist. Not even from a donor.

It was from the National Muslim Civic Engagement Alliance, a quiet but powerful network based in D.C. They'd watched the rise and fall of Black Up from a distance, and now, they were paying close attention to what we were building.

The subject line read:

"We'd like to invite you to consider national partnership."

Inside, the message was brief but heavy.

_Brother Jibril,

Your recent community strategy and leadership framework has caught our attention. We'd like to speak with you about expanding your initiative beyond Houston.

Specifically, we're considering appointing a Southern Regional Director—someone who can oversee and mentor local organizers while representing a new era of Muslim civic leadership.

We believe you're already doing the work. We'd like to resource you to do it nationally.

– M.A., Executive Director

National Muslim Civic Engagement Alliance_

My chest tightened.

This was the kind of opportunity that could change everything—funding, staffing, political capital, policy access. But it also came with something else: scrutiny. Bureaucracy. The kind of machine that chews up grassroots spirit and spits out statistics.

I forwarded the email to no one.

Instead, I printed it. Folded it. And took it with me to jummah.

That Friday, the khutbah was about sincerity—how intention is what defines legacy in Islam. Not the size of your following. Not the praise. Not the press.

Just niyyah.

After prayer, I sat with the Imam. A wise, quiet Sudanese elder who never asked for recognition, yet somehow knew everything.

"Do you think it's wrong to lead more people if it means compromising a little?" I asked.

He didn't answer immediately. He looked out the masjid window for a while, then finally said, "The Prophet led a nation without ever lying to gain influence. Start there."

That night, I told Sara about the offer.

She didn't blink. "Do it if it aligns. Decline it if it distracts. But don't sell your soul to rent a microphone."

So I asked myself:

Was this a platform to uplift the mission? Or a trap to water it down?

The next morning, I replied:

_Thank you for the honor.

I'd be happy to collaborate, consult, and even travel when needed.

But if your plan requires me to stop walking with my people on the ground in order to represent them from above, I'm not your guy.

I'm still on the sidewalk.

That's where I plan to stay._

The next morning, I woke up before the adhan.

No alarm.

Just something pulling at my ribs—the kind of tug you get when you've finally stopped running from your purpose long enough to hear it call your name.

The house was still.

Sara was asleep, curled beside one of the twins who had snuck into our bed sometime after midnight. Imani's backpack was already packed for her Saturday Qur'an class, sitting by the door like a little act of faith in routine.

I stepped out onto the porch.

The sky was still a navy hush, not yet willing to give up the stars. But the horizon—it was thinking about something. The pink, the orange, the slow breath of light beginning to stretch.

It felt familiar.

The way beginnings feel when you've already survived so many endings. Behind me was everything we'd built: the bruised friendships, the quiet betrayals, the women who held the community together without applause, the brothers who stayed even when everything told them to leave.

Ahead of me?

That was the beautiful part.

I didn't know.

And I didn't need to.

Because what we had now wasn't just a second chance.

It was a right start.

Not perfect. But righteous.

Not loud. But lasting.

I took out my phone—not to scroll, not to check messages—but to text three names:

Bronx. Bilal. Soraya.

Just one sentence.

Sun's coming up. Let's meet soon.

I didn't say where. I didn't say why.

Because if they knew anything, it was this:

Movements don't end when the noise dies down.

They rise when the people are still willing to walk—even when it's quiet.

And I was ready to walk again.

Not for a headline.

Not for a legacy.

But for my people.

For my family.

For the ones coming after.

The sun rose, slow and golden.

And I rose with it.